Honour Bound

Wendy Cartmell

Costa Press

DEDICATION

For my children
Holly and Ben

Rape

Rape is not merely violation with a sexual reference, it is much more; it is an assault by intimate physical violence, it is extreme aggressive bullying and an act of oppression. It is a crime where the victims are often found guilty by their peers and carries a lifelong stigma.

Anon

Chapter 1

At 11pm on Saturday night Sgt Major Crane was on the streets of Aldershot. Flashing blue lights ripped through the night, bizarrely revolving in time to music throbbing out of the open pub doors. Young men were shouting lewd remarks across the street to clutches of girls helping each other totter home on their impossibly high heels. The local kebab shop was doing a roaring trade in food purchased on a whim and then discarded after the first bite. Greasy wrapping paper spread like confetti around the overflowing refuse bins.

Crane spotted a body sprawled half in the road and half on the kerb. The girl's dress, if you could call it that, Crane thought was hitched up around her hips showing flesh spilling out of a tiny thong. A pool of vomit lay close to her face. Crane averted his gaze and nodded to a young woman police officer who went to her aid. She coaxed the girl upright, removing her shoes when it became obvious she couldn't balance on her cheap Jimmy Choo rip offs. After a quick conversation she pointed her in the direction of the traffic lights at the bottom of the road. The girl drifted away, shoes in hand, but no handbag or coat. Crane knew there was no point in calling her a taxi as drivers won't take those likely to throw up in their car. Crane wondered if she had her house keys, but then decided that as the girl was clearly too far gone to care, why should he? He found it hard to muster sympathy for her plight. After all, as far as he was concerned, it was self inflicted. He shook his head in dismay, at the lack of self respect displayed by the young people around him.

Crane lit a cigarette and wandered over to DI Anderson of the local Aldershot Police. "Jesus, Derek, what a bloody mess."

For once Crane was referring to something other than Anderson's grey wispy hair.

"Tell me about it, Crane. This bloody lot costs us a fortune, what with extra officers on the beat and overtime. Anyway, what are you doing with a cigarette in your hand? I thought you were going to give up when the baby was born?"

"Well, you know how it is. I've cut down a lot though, no smoking at home, that sort of thing."

"What does Tina say about that?"

"Nothing, as long as I don't smoke around the baby. That's her main concern at the moment. The baby." Crane took a long noisy drag on his cigarette.

"Well, it will be. Feeling a bit left out are you?"

Crane didn't answer the question, choosing instead to grind his cigarette out under his shoe. "Right, I'm off now. Are we agreed that the problem here is booze not drugs?"

"Definitely. There are always a few tablets floating around, but nothing serious. Most of the kids just do booze. I don't think they can afford both."

"Okay, I'll report back to Captain Edwards on Monday and hopefully I won't have to do another

Saturday night stint here. Bloody idiots, I don't know how you stand it."

Crane nodded his head at the police officers still dealing with the sea of humanity breaking out of the pub doors in waves.

"Oh, right, so you don't get drunk then?" Anderson snorted. "What about all your ceremonial dinners? I hear they disintegrate into wild nights once you're all tanked up."

"Maybe they do, Derek. The difference is, we keep it on the Garrison and the wives dress like women not whores."

Crane turned and marched off in the direction of his car, leaving the destruction behind him, not noticing Anderson's smile.

Chapter 2

The wailing cut through Crane's dream like a knife, plunging him awake, as though he had been ducked into a freezing cold bath. Instinct took over and within seconds he was out of bed and at his son's side. Picking up the soaking baby from the cot, he held him close, while they both calmed down. He was going to have to stop reacting like this, he knew, but well, it was his military training. At the first scream, his instincts took over and he was in the other room before conscious thought kicked in.

"You beat me to it again then," Tina's eyes were glazed with exhaustion as she leaned on the side of the bedroom door, trying to push her greasy dishevelled long black hair off her wan face. The baggy t-shirt she slept in failing to hide the sagging flesh around her waist and stomach, left over from her pregnancy.

"Sorry, I just…sorry." Crane didn't know what else to say to make the situation any better, so settled for, "Look, you sort yourself out and I'll clean him up and bring him through in a minute," falling back on his army training, making sure everything was in order. At six thirty in the morning he simply couldn't deal with emotional stuff.

Tina nodded and turned to go into the bathroom. Crane thought she looked too exhausted to even manage a conversion.

As he changed his son's nappy he noticed the once organised nursery was a mess. After they'd decorated the small room, Crane put shelves up over the changing table to hold all the baby paraphernalia, so everything was on hand for Tina. But his system didn't work unless items were put back in their correct place and so instead of being a symphony of order, it had become a discord of disorder. The same was true of the rest of the room. Drawers were half closed with baby clothes peeping from them, the small wardrobe doors were swinging open and in the rubbish bin were too many used disposable nappies in sacks. Glancing at the clock on the wall, he thought he should just have time to tidy up and restock the shelves before he went to work. Now they'd moved back onto Aldershot Garrison and rented out the house they owned in Ash, it only took a few minutes for Crane to reach Provost Barracks, where the Branch were based.

Once Daniel was clean and dry, yet still gulping back sobs and trying to stuff his fists into his mouth as though they'd provide the nourishment he needed, Crane carried the baby through to the bedroom. Whilst Daniel was happily feeding, Crane had a quick shower, made coffee and then tidied up the nursery. When he popped his head back into the bedroom mother and son were sleeping. Deciding to leave them well alone, Crane went back downstairs and left a note for Tina, before heading out.

Their army quarter was a fairly new link-detached house, the small estate built to resemble a civvy housing estate, rather than the bleak council estate type of older Garrison properties. Crane had ignored jibes of 'lucky sod' and 'do you have to be in the Branch to get one of those then?' The houses were prized amongst the ranks and Crane's neighbours were of the same standing in the army – Sergeants and Warrant Officers only. The army doing their usual trick of keeping each rank separate as much as possible.

Tina was very upset about leaving their lovely old Victorian semi in Ash, but the budget just hadn't added up. Without her salary, they couldn't keep up the mortgage payments, feed and clothe themselves and buy all the necessary baby things. So, as they'd got a good long term rental, they moved back onto the Garrison. Crane hoped Tina would embrace army life more than she had at the moment. Perhaps she would once the baby was a bit older. As it was, he didn't think she's coping, but that was a problem for another day. Now he had to concentrate on his report to his superior, Captain Edwards, about his findings on Saturday night.

As Crane returned from the meeting later that morning, Sgt Kim Weston, the SIB Office Manager called him over.

"Sir, I've had a call from DI Anderson. He wants you to go over to Aldershot Police Station."

"Any idea why Kim?"

"He asked that you go as soon you were out of your meeting. He has a possible new case, but wouldn't give me any details." Kim's uniform, hair and desk were as pristine as ever and she was reading the message from her ever present notebook. Her long blond hair was scraped back from her face and tied neatly in a bun at the nape of her neck.

"Thanks, Kim, in that case you're with me, Billy."

"Boss," Sgt Billy Williams said, grabbing his suit jacket from the back of his chair, as they went to the car.

The short drive, along Queens Avenue, down Hospital Hill, and finally circumventing Aldershot town up towards the police station, only took about five minutes. But it took just as long once they had arrived, for Crane to find a parking space in the overcrowded car park.

As Billy and Crane got out of the car, the cold early October wind rushed through the tunnel of walkways leading to the town centre, tugging at their clothes and hair. Crane's close cropped dark hair didn't move, but Billy's shock of blond hair fell over his forehead. One final huff of wind pushed them through the front door and they arrived amid a swirl of leaves and debris, in the foyer of Aldershot Police Station. They showed their passes to the bored Desk Sergeant and were allowed through to CID.

"Well, if it isn't the Men in Black," DI Anderson called to Crane and Billy as they reached his office door. Anderson's joke was wearing a bit thin as far as Crane was concerned. It was a reference to the fact that Branch investigators don't wear army uniform and so Crane and Billy had swopped one uniform for another. They both wore dark suits and white shirts, normally sporting Regimental ties. The only concession being short sleeved shirts in the summer and long sleeved ones in the winter.

"Ha ha, Derek, very droll," said Crane as he brushed some shrivelled brown leaves from his hair. "So what have you got for us?"

"Not a very nice case, I'm afraid. Come on in, I've got copies of the paperwork for you."

Crane and Billy squeezed into Anderson's office, which looked as though the wind from downstairs had been playing havoc in it. Billy stood by the door as there was only one free chair which Crane took; the other one being buried under piles of files. The waste paper basket sported a decorative ring of crumpled paper. Derek himself looks like he'd had an argument with the icy blast and the blast won. His prematurely grey wispy hair, which should be wrapped around his bald spot, was standing on end. His jacket was discarded on the floor and his once clean tie was loosely tied around a collar frayed from use. However, many an Aldershot villain, to their detriment, had mistaken his sloppy appearance as a reflection of his work.

"I'm afraid we've got a rather disturbing case of rape and murder, Crane," Anderson explained. "A young girl, Becca Henderson, was attacked on Saturday night. It seems she met a boy in The Goose pub, had her drink spiked and was then taken back to her own flat, where she was raped and murdered."

Anderson handed over the file and Crane flicked through it with Billy looking over his shoulder.

"Was a full rape kit examination done?" Crane asked.

"Yes, during the autopsy yesterday. Things are a bit quiet over at Frimley Park Hospital at the moment, so they did it straight away. Forensics went over her flat, but there's nothing of any help so far. Not even a bloody fingerprint. This one was definitely premeditated. He coldly picked her out, picked her up and then drugged her. He had the audacity to tell her friends he would help her get safely back to her flat, but once there he raped then killed her, all without leaving anything behind."

"Well," Crane said, handing the file over his shoulder to Billy, "it's very sad and all that, but look at what the girl was wearing." Crane was referring to the crime scene photographs. "Look at her clothes. They barely covered her body. She may as well have been naked. She might as well have had a red light shining above her head, for God's sake, telling any bloke that fancied a bit, that she was available."

"Jesus, Crane, that's harsh. The girl didn't ask to be raped and killed," Anderson looked aghast.

"I'm not saying she did, Derek, but I was with you out there on Saturday night, if you remember and none of the girls acted as though they had one bit of self restraint. They put themselves into vulnerable situations without a second thought. Anyway, what's it got to do with us? By the sounds of it, it could have been anyone."

"Because one witness, the girl's best friend, reckons the bloke who did it was a squaddie," snapped Anderson.

That shut Crane up and wiped the smirk off Billy's face.

Chapter 3

The smoke from Crane's cigarette was drifting away towards the playing fields located on the opposite side of Queens Avenue, in front of Provost Barracks. Which was precisely what Crane was doing, drifting away, thinking. As he smoked with one hand, the other was fingering the mobile phone in his pocket. His guilty pin was poking into his brain, saying he should phone to check that Tina and Daniel were alright. But he couldn't get out of his head random thoughts of rape and murder. He saw again the pubescent girls from last Saturday night, giggling with their friends, flashing pretty eyes at young soldiers. Not understanding the danger they were putting themselves in. Not thinking that anything bad could happen. Innocents, who had been seduced by pop videos into wearing inappropriate clothing.

Did he see Becca that night? He took his hand off his mobile phone and pulled out of his jacket pocket a photograph of her and studied it. No, he didn't think so. But then again, a lot of the girls looked the same that night. Clones, fashioned from pages in magazines. He knew the words he blurted out in Anderson's office were out of order. Perhaps there was nothing wrong in the youngsters having a good time in their own way. Maybe he was just getting too old. Unable to remember what he was like when he was their age. Crane smiled sardonically to himself. Well, maybe he could remember, just doesn't want to admit that he was just as bad, in his time.

Turning back to the photograph, he wondered if he had seen the boy who killed her. The one supposed to be a soldier. Crane shook his head in frustration. Fuck knows. But one thing he did know was that standing there wasn't achieving anything. So dropping his cigarette butt on the floor, he placed his foot over it, crushing it as he turned and walked away.

Entering the SIB office, he called for Billy and Kim to join him and they dutifully followed him into his lair, Kim bringing with her a welcome mug of coffee for him. Crane's domain was a small room with no space for luxuries such as a conference table, so he sat behind his desk, with Billy and Kim taking the only other chairs in the room. Billy lounged rather than sat, his broad muscular frame threatening to break the cheap chair. Kim seemingly sat to attention, her notebook open and pen poised.

Crane looked down at the photograph which was still in his hand, turned it around and pushed it across the desk towards Billy and Kim.

"Right, this rape and murder of Becca Henderson, we need to decide on a way forward."

"Are you sure it's a soldier then, boss?"

"No one's sure of anything, Billy, but we have a duty to see what we can do from this end. Any ideas Kim?"

"Yes, sir, I thought I'd take a look at the description from the witnesses and put it into the computer. Do a search and see who I find."

"Just about the whole bloody Garrison, eh, boss?"

"That doesn't mean I shouldn't do it, Sgt Williams."

The lining of Kim's uniform skirt hissed as she crossed her legs, as though at outward sign of her displease with Billy.

"No it doesn't, Kim. What about you, Billy? Have you any thoughts about the way forward?"

Billy sat upright, "Well, I know it's a bit off the wall, boss, but what if there have been other cases of rape or rape and murder in other Garrison towns?"

"Oh, so now we're looking for a serial rapist?" Kim flipped a page in her notebook.

"For God's sake you two, cut it out."

Crane picked up his coffee mug and hid his smile.

"Two good ideas so off you go. Oh," he called as his two Sergeants rose to leave, "go back say three years for both searches."

As Kim left the office, Billy hung back, asking for a quiet word.

"Of course, Billy, what is it?"

Billy closed the door but remained standing next to it.

"Well, it's this rape business, boss."

"And?"

"Well, it's just that…" Billy pushed his blond hair away from his forehead.

"Bloody hell, come and sit down and spit it out. I won't bite."

Billy did as he was told. Placing his elbows on his open legs and hanging his head, he looked between his hands at the carpet. For once Crane decided to keep quiet. Something was definitely wrong. Billy was normally over confident, but at the moment was being strangely reticent.

"I've got this mate, met him at the gym. He seems to be in a bit of trouble," he mumbled to the floor. Then lifted his head and looked around the office, anywhere other than at Crane, who didn't comment.

"He's one of us, you know, not an MP or anything, just your regular squaddie."

Billy was faltering, so Crane had to prompt, "And?"

"And it's just with this rape stuff…"

Crane leaned forwards over his desk, "Billy, are you trying to tell me you think this mate of yours might be our rapist?"

This time Billy did look at Crane, "No sir, I'm trying to tell you that he's been repeatedly raped. Here on the Garrison, by a fellow soldier."

A Letter to my Rapist

I'm not sure how to start this letter. The term 'Dear Rapist' has a certain ring to it, but then again you are certainly not my 'dear' anything. How about 'Dear sir'? The 'sir' bit is about right but the 'dear' is still wrong. So I think I will leave out the salutation and just get on with it.

I wanted to share one of my flashbacks with you. Just to give you some idea of how you are making me feel. I'm sure you couldn't care less, but putting pen to paper helps me, so you'll just have to put up with it, the same as I have.

I can be anywhere when a flashback happens. Luckily most times are when I'm alone in my room. It happened on Guard Duty once though. That was a bit dodgy. I had to pretend I had a bad stomach. How else could I explain my vomiting?

It starts with uncontrollable shivers. Then the memories come. Settling on me like snow. Chilling my body, heart and soul, as I relive the horror of that first time. As I feel again the terror rendering me voiceless, my gaping mouth unable to scream, speak or even whimper, as though I had been struck dumb. I'm aware of the familiar khaki of my tunic, scratching at my cheek, as I am roughly pounded from above. A draft from the open window mocks me, playing across my bare legs, teasing the hairs and kissing my skin like a lover. Then the unbelievable pain that unlocks my voice as my skin tears and I scream like a girl, until a sweaty sock is stuffed into my gaping mouth.

But nothing lasts forever and once you are satisfied, there is a single sharp splinter of pain as I am released.

"I told you you'd enjoy it," your deep voice whispers, as my own body offers the final betrayal.

Chapter 4

Crane believed he was the master of lobbing metaphorical grenades, but had to admit that one from Billy was right there up with the best of them. Sweet Jesus. Not only a squaddie being accused of rape and murder in Aldershot, but now a young male soldier being raped and on Crane's Garrison. It was unbelievable. The lad didn't seem to want to make an official complaint yet, so Crane and Billy would have to tread very carefully on this one. Well, as carefully as Crane could. He was not very good at treading carefully, he had to admit to himself.

This was the first case of this type Crane had ever investigated. Male rape. It was one of those incidents that people knew must happen, not just in the army, but in all three forces, hell even in 'civvy street'. But it was simply not talked about. There were very few official complaints and those soldiers who did make the decision to press charges, were often as humiliated by the process as they were by their tormentor.

Crane couldn't begin to imagine the stress the poor bloke must be under, this must surely be beyond his capacity to cope, making him feel threatened - not only by his rapist but also by the system. By those who are supposed to help him. He must be fighting a hell of a battle with his anxiety and fear to follow through with an official complaint. Crane shuddered at the thought of the physical attacks the young soldier had been subjected to. That sort of physical violation would surely drive a man mad.

As these jumbled thoughts whizzed around his brain, Crane parked the car outside his quarter and entered the house. It was only when he realised there were no cooking smells greeting him, no soft lighting and the house felt cold, that he stopped thinking about work.

His first thought was, where's Tina? His second, is Daniel alright? Quickly followed by the outlandish thought - she hasn't left me has she? After checking the downstairs rooms, in a manner reminiscent of clearing a house of opponents, Crane headed for the stairs, taking them two at a time. He burst into the nursery - only to find it empty. Fighting his rising panic, he sprinted into his bedroom, drawing in a deep breath.

His shout of, "Tina!" died on his lips, as he spied his wife and son fast asleep in the large double bed. Walking into the room, he saw a note on the bedside table from Tina. 'Sorry, so tired. Wake me up when you get home'.

Crane looked down on his sleeping wife, waiting while his heart rate slowed and his breathing returned to normal. I have to get her some help, he realised as he kneeled by the bed and woke her by kissing her face and stroking her hair, careful not to disturb Daniel. As she blinked awake, she muttered, "Tom? Is that you?"

"Yes, love."

"Sorry, is it that time already, I've slept longer than I meant to, I've got to get up, I need to make something for dinner, sorry." Tina struggled to sit up with Daniel still in her arms.

"It's okay, I'll take Daniel." Crane lifted the baby and put him over his shoulder. "I'll put him in his cot as he's still asleep. Why don't you have a shower while I cook dinner? I'll see you downstairs when you're ready."

He left the room before Tina could refuse his help. She had been doing a lot of that lately, refusing his help. But Crane could see by the pallor of her skin, the dark smudges under her eyes and unwashed hair, that she was clearly not coping. The baby stirred once in his arms and then settled again and Crane managed to get Daniel back into his cot without waking him. A quick sweep of the nursery confirmed that it needed tidying again, so muttering under his breath, he did just that. A few minutes later, as Crane clattered down the stairs, he heard the water running in the bathroom.

With Tina and Daniel sorted, Crane opened the fridge, ready to try out his non-existent culinary skills. But the contents didn't look promising. A wedge of old cheese, a couple of eggs, some left over vegetables and a litre of milk. Not enough ingredients to make a cheese omelette for two, which was his usual attempt at a meal. So Crane grabbed the phone and ordered a large take-away pizza to be delivered. He then went through the house, turning on lights, turning up the heating and opening a bottle of wine.

By the time Tina came down, he was sipping a beer, with the pizza keeping warm in the oven.

"Did I just hear the doorbell?" Tina asked.

"Doorbell? No I don't think so. Here sit down; I've

19

poured you a glass of wine and dinner's ready," Crane said producing the pizza with a flourish, still in the Dominoes Pizza box.

"You silly bugger," Tina laughed and held up her glass. "Do you think I should drink this as I'm still breastfeeding the baby?"

"Tina, I'm sure a small glass of wine won't hurt."

Taking a sip of her drink, she said, "Mm that's nice, thanks, Tom."

"Oh it was nothing, I only had to pick up the phone and place an order."

"You know what I mean. Thanks for helping and I'm sorry…"

Crane cut in. "That's enough of that. Normally it's me saying sorry. Don't you get into the habit as well; otherwise we'll never get anywhere."

They managed to eat most of the pizza before the baby monitor squawked. Daniel telling them it was his turn to eat.

"Sorry," mumbled Tina, as she rushed out of the room.

Crane sat alone for a while finishing the last slice of pizza and thinking about Tina for once, rather than work. As he did so, he unconsciously rubbed the scar under his beard - a red angry souvenir from shrapnel in Afghanistan, which he had collected whilst training members of the Afghan Police Force. Surrounded by an empty pizza box, empty beer can and half drunk glass of wine, Crane came to a decision and picked up his mobile phone.

Chapter 5

The following morning, DI Anderson was waiting for Crane, as he ran up the wide concrete steps fronting the shabby Victorian house.

"Thanks for meeting me, Derek," Crane said as he wrapped his dark coat around him against the cold wind, taking care not to bend the large brown envelope he was holding.

"It's okay, I know how you like to view the scene and anyway, a fresh pair of eyes can't do any harm."

"Don't know about fresh," Crane sighed, rubbing his eyes to make his point, stopping just short of a yawn.

"For goodness sake, pull yourself together, Crane. You're not the only man in the world with a new baby in the house."

Realising he'd get no sympathy from Anderson, who was a father of two girls, Crane looked around the area. The terraced houses were on a street which had been an affluent area when the houses were first built. Now they were too large and expensive for families to buy and maintain and had therefore mostly been broken up into flats and bedsits. Looking over the railing of the steps,

Crane saw a basement flat instead of a garden. Tilting his head back, Crane realised the houses were three storeys, a basement, ground and first floors.

Anderson fished around for the bunch of keys, patting each of his pockets before finding it. He pushed a key into the lock on the large, scratched and scuffed green front door, opening it into a small hall area. On their left hand side was a door marked Flat 2. Anderson unlocked this, easily pushing open the flimsy plywood door and stepping back. "This is the one," he said, rather unnecessarily.

"Thanks, give me a minute, would you?"

As Anderson turned and wandered back outside, Crane stepped into the small flat and pushed the door closed behind him, muffling, but not cutting out completely, the noise of the traffic filtering through from outside. Actually 'flat' was a generous description, Crane decided. Bedsit was more like it. As he looked around the room, the double bed dominated, drawing the eye. Opening the envelope he was holding, Crane removed large photographs of the crime scene. The bed dominated these as well and they showed a young girl lying on top of it.

Crane took a few steps to the bed, fanning out the photographs on the now empty mattress. He placed them in order. The first was a close-up of Becca's face, eyes open wide, staring, yet sightless. Eye makeup smeared. Lips faintly stained red from lipstick. The second photo showed her neck, bruised from the hands that throttled the life out of her.

Carefully placing the third one in position, Crane looked at Becca's bare breasts. Caught underneath her body, the remnants of the top the killer had ripped from her could just be seen. The fourth showed a close-up of her from her waist to the tops of her legs. A small skirt now reminiscent of a belt, bunched up around her waist. Below that she was naked, bare legs splayed.

The two remaining glossy pictures were of each leg, one of them was dangling off the edge of the bed. She was still wearing her shoes.

Leaving the pictures in place on the bed, Crane straightened up and looked around. A large bay window was covered by curtains that were closed and underneath it were a small TV and digital receiver. The bed split the room in two and over on the far wall was a small kitchen area. Rounding the bed Crane walked over and saw another door. Pushing it open he revealed a small bathroom. The toilet, sink and shower were all covered in black fingerprint powder. Returning to the bed, Crane stood still and listened. The only sound was the slight humming of a small fridge in the kitchen.

Crane tried to imagine this small space alive with a young girl getting ready for a night out with her friends, but found it impossible. The killer had sucked the life out of the bedsit as surely as he had sucked the life out of Becca.

Collecting the photographs, Crane opened the door and joined Anderson in the hall.

"No useful forensic evidence?" Crane asked, although he already knew the answer.

"Not a bloody thing. No finger prints, no hair, no semen. Just traces of lubricant from a condom. No wrappers, cigarette butts, empty glasses he drank from. No hairs in the sink, down the plug holes or in the drain pipes. No…"

"Alright, Derek, I get the picture. The forensic team have done a thorough job and came up with nothing."

"That's about right."

Anderson closed and double locked the door to Flat 2. Moving through the front door and standing on the steps he said, "The only thing we've got is the witness who swears the bloke was a squaddie."

"Well that link is a bit tenuous to say the least."

Crane joined Anderson on the steps and stuffed his hands into the pocket of his coat. His new tactic, aimed at stopping him lighting a cigarette.

"Why? Because you don't want it to be one of your lads?" Derek patted down his hair, which was being blown about by the cold wind.

"Not at all, Derek," Crane walked down the steps. "It's because it's such a generic description. Your so called witness can't really help with colour of hair, eyes, height or build, can she? And she was drunk at the time. And it was in a crowded pub with dim lights and blaring music."

"Well, as it's the only thing I've got at the moment, I'm running with it. So on Saturday night I'll be going around the bars talking to doormen and taxi drivers. I need to find anyone who saw Becca last week. Why don't you come too? Maybe then we can start filling in some of your blanks."

Chapter 6

Crane's superior officer, Captain Edwards, was not happy. Actually, Crane thought that was an understatement. Edwards was furious. And all Crane had done was to tell him about the two rape cases.

"So, let me see if I've got this right," Edwards said tersely, standing behind his desk and peering down at Crane, who was sitting on the other side. "You're firstly telling me that a young girl, Becca Henderson, was raped and murdered last Saturday night and Aldershot Police thinks a squaddie was the culprit."

"Yes, sir," Crane replied just to get up Edwards' long nose.

"And secondly," Edwards continued, ignoring the interruption, "Billy has reported a conversation with one Private Sebastian Turner, who has confessed to being raped by a fellow soldier." Edwards pushed his straight black hair from his deep forehead.

"Yes, sir."

"Dear God, whatever is the British Army coming to?" Edwards fumbled behind him, grabbed his chair and sank into it. "There is nothing I hate more than rape cases. Very sensitive issues involved and they can be very hard to prove. So, over to you, Crane, I think. Tell me what you're going to do about them."

Crane once again noted Edwards' trick of demanding answers without offering any investigative insight.

"Well, sir, I'm going out with DI Anderson again on Saturday night, this time to question the doormen at the local pubs and the taxi drivers. To see if we can find anyone who saw Becca that night or, more importantly, saw her rapist."

"What's his description?" Edwards leaned forwards to listen.

Crane opened his folder and read from a witness statement. Actually the only witness statement they had so far. "A witness described him and I quote verbatim, 'He was, like, tallish. I think his hair was blond, or blondish. I reckon he was a squaddie. After all, The Goose is a squaddie pub, innit?' I'm not altogether sure if that last bit about The Goose was a question or a statement, sir."

"Come again?"

Crane began to read the statement once more.

"Shut up, Crane," Edwards interrupted. "Is DI Anderson really taking this witness seriously?"

"At the moment, sir, I don't think he has much choice. It's the only thing he has. No forensics at all I'm afraid. No finger prints, blood,"

"Yes, yes, Crane, I know what forensics are, thank you."

Crane hid a surreptitious smile behind a coffee cup he put to his lips.

"What about the other case?" Captain Edwards leaned so far back in his chair that Crane thought he was in danger of falling over backwards. It was as if

Edwards was trying to get as far away from the cases as he could.

"Well, sir, at the moment there's very little I can do. Turner hasn't made a formal complaint, but Billy is pretty sure he will. Until then, we just have to wait. I was thinking about doing some background checks, sir."

"Background checks on Turner you mean?"

"Yes, sir, but also the other men in his Company, especially his superiors. If anything, it's more likely a Corporal or Lance Corporal that's doing this to him, someone with authority over him."

Edwards sat up straight. "I think you're right on that one, Crane," he said. "But you can't go around doing background checks until a formal complaint is made. So keep that line of enquiry until Turner spills the beans. Understood?"

"Perfectly, sir."

"Very well, dismissed."

Crane took the stairs down to SIB two at a time. Banging through the double doors, he called for Kim to join him in his office.

"Right, Kim, a job for you on the Turner case. I want to make sure we're prepared for when he makes a formal complaint."

"Sir," Kim acknowledged, opening her notebook.

"I want the records for the other Privates in his Unit and his immediate Corporal and Lance Corporal."

"Very well, sir. Whose authority do I log as granting permission for retrieving the information?"

"Why, Captain Edwards, of course," Crane managed to say with a straight face.

A letter to Billy

Dear Billy

This time I can start a letter properly, but you don't need to know about that. This is a thank you letter really. I wanted to say thanks for listening when I blurted out my problems and for not running away as I confessed to what was happening to me. But as I recall, it was me that ran away wasn't it? I know I'll have to stop that if I want this thing to come to an end - running away that is.

But I'm not sure if I have the courage yet to go through with giving you the name of my violator. The man who has crashed into my life and taken it over. The one who reduces me to a gibbering wreck. The person who has made me afraid of my own shadow.

He's very clever. He knows it's the uncertainty that I find so frightening. The uncertainty that makes me jump if I hear a deep voice in the corridor outside my room. Is that him? Is he coming tonight?

I used to stay around people as much as I could, safety in numbers and all that. But now I'm sure they can tell. I'm sure that they know, somehow, that I am less of a man than them. So now I shy away from my colleagues, which, in turn, makes me more isolated and vulnerable.

I am trying hard to get a grip on my emotions. When I do, I'll be strong enough to name him and face my shame. But I'm just not there yet.

Sorry.

Chapter 7

Saturday night found Crane back on duty in Aldershot town centre with DI Anderson.

"We must stop meeting like this," Anderson quipped as they took the short walk from the car park to the centre of town.

For once it was Anderson marching along and Crane lagging behind. The cold night air bit after the warmth of the car, making Crane even more fed up.

"Bloody hell, Derek, how come you're so happy to be in Aldershot on a Saturday night?" he grumbled.

"Oh stop being so grumpy, Crane. What's the matter with you now?" Anderson stopped and waited for Crane to catch him up.

"Sorry, it's just that I don't like leaving Tina too much at the moment. Not more than I have to."

Crane stopped to light a cigarette, giving into the craving. Sod putting his hands in his pockets, he thought.

"By the way, thank Jean for her visit, will you?" he asked once he'd taken that first all important drag.

"It did the trick then?"

"Did it ever. At least now Tina isn't trying to kill

herself by breastfeeding the baby all the time. She took Jean's advice, that there's no shame in not producing enough milk for a three month old and has started bottle feeding Daniel. He just wasn't satisfied by the amount of milk Tina was producing. So now I can take my turn giving him a bottle. It's definitely made a difference to her. Well, to both of us, actually."

"Glad to hear it," said Anderson. "So can we get on with the job now?" and he picked up his pace again, heading for the plethora of bars clustered around Victoria Street.

The 'job' involved talking to doormen, bouncers and taxi drivers, to see if anyone remembered Becca from last week. Anderson had managed to get a good head and shoulders photograph of Becca from her parents, so they didn't have to show a picture of her dead. Always a plus, thought Crane, looking at the shot of Becca smiling into the camera, taken on a day out somewhere on the South Coast.

As they strolled up the street, avoiding the debris, swaying girls and staggering boys, they stopped at each pub in turn including Yates and the Queen Victoria and talked to the doormen. Unfortunately they got the same response everywhere.

"No, mate, sorry not seen her before."

"They all look the same to me, pal."

"She's not here tonight. Could you move along, you're putting off the punters!"

Crane decided that most of them were as thick as their biceps. When they got to The Goose, they flashed their badges and went inside.

"Oy, you," Anderson called to a young man working behind the bar, "over here."

Anderson put his credentials and the picture of

Becca on the bar, under the young man's nose.

"Did you see this girl last Saturday night?"

"Sorry, never seen her before." The lad's words come out slurred because of the tongue piercing he was sporting. His face was flushed from the heat, not only from the bodies crushed inside the pub, but also from all the chillers behind the bar. There were gleaming glass upright fridges lined up against the wall, filled with equally gleaming bottles of alcho-pops, in all colours of the rainbow, each one more enticing than the last. Pieces of fluorescent coloured card encouraged their binge drinking clients to buy, proclaiming 'TWO FOR THE PRICE OF ONE!'

"Think about it," Crane urged, wanting to bat the barman around the head to encourage his co-operation, but restraining himself. "Are you sure you didn't see her last Saturday?"

"I don't need to think, mate, I wasn't here."

"Well, who the bloody hell was?" Crane shouted, firstly from anger and secondly to make himself heard over the thumping music.

"Um, let me think, oh yeah, Simon was."

"And where is Simon?" Anderson wanted to know.

"He's covering the other end of the bar, he's the one with a blond streak in his hair. Now can I get on with serving, before I lose my job? I don't like it much, but I need the money, see?"

Not bothering to reply, Crane and Anderson threaded their way through the crowd of revellers to the other end of the pub.

'Blond Streak' as Crane dubbed Simon the moment he saw him, managed to impart some information as he continued pouring drinks and taking money.

"Yeah, I remember her, a bit tasty innit? So why do

you lot want to know about her? Been flashing it around for money, has she?"

Ignoring the question, Anderson pressed on. "Did you see who she was with that night?"

"Yeah, she was with some new bloke. I've never seen him before, so I was interested like. Thanks darling," he winked at a pretty dark-haired girl he'd just taken money from.

"Can you describe him?"

"Probably, but why? Is he her pimp?" Simon nodded at a customer to acknowledge an order and grabbed a pint glass, starting to fill it with beer.

"More than likely, her murderer," Crane chipped in.

"Bloody hell!"

Crane wasn't sure if the expletive was because of the fact that Becca was dead, or because Blond Streak had dropped the glass he was filling in shock.

"I need you to report to Aldershot Police Station at nine o'clock tomorrow morning to give a statement and description," Anderson demanded.

"Have a heart; I don't knock off here until two."

"Alright, eleven o'clock, but don't be late, or a police constable will be calling at your flat to arrest you."

As Anderson took down Blond Streak's contact details, Crane watched the punters in the pub. The girls still all looked the same to him. Barbie dolls, all tits and short skirts. As he eyed a particularly raucous table of girls he noticed one of them was more reserved.

"Bloody hell, its Kim," he said to Anderson, nudging him and pointing her out. "I wonder what she's doing here."

"Trying to have a good time and failing, by the looks of her. Leave her alone, Crane. Don't embarrass her by going over. The last thing she needs is to be singled out by both the police and her boss."

"I guess you're right," Crane said, turning away. "Come on let's get out of here."

The last people on their list were the taxi drivers. Sauntering over to the rank, they approached the first car in the long line.

"Where to, mate?"

"Nowhere and I am not your mate," Crane growled pushing the photo of Becca though the driver's window. "Were you working last Saturday night? Did you see this girl?"

This was repeated at every taxi, without any success.

Walking back to the car park, Crane and Anderson agreed to meet again on Monday morning, so Anderson could bring Crane up to date with the description from Blond Streak. With a wave goodbye to Derek, Crane pulled out of the car park, glad to be away from the frenzied activity of the town centre. As he drove away, he nearly knocked over a tall dark-haired lad, sprinting across the road towards The Goose.

Chapter 8

By four o'clock on Sunday afternoon, Crane was lying on the settee with Daniel across his chest. They were both dozing. Crane because he had just eaten his first roast dinner in ages that he and Tina had cooked together and Daniel because Crane has just given him a bottle of milk. In Crane's dream the mobile phone in his pocket was ringing and vibrating against his leg. Dragging it out and looking at the caller ID, he saw it was a call from Kim. Answering he barked, "Yes, Sgt Weston?" wondering why she would be calling him. He was clearly on holiday. He could even see the sea from his prone position on a sun bed.

"Sorry to bother you on a Sunday, sir, but I need a bit of help, I'm afraid."

"Help, Kim? What sort of …."

Crane was dragged from his dream by the phone call and by Daniel crying. Juggling the baby and the mobile, Crane sat up, the leather of the settee creaking in protest.

"Hang on a minute, Kim; I'll give the baby to Tina. She's just arrived."

Passing the baby into her outstretched arms, Crane

waited until Tina and Daniel had left the room, before continuing his conversation.

"Sorry, Kim, right, what's the matter?"

"I need you to come to my flat, sir, preferably with DI Anderson."

"When? Why?" Crane was still half asleep and couldn't get his head around why Kim would want him to go over, never mind with DI Anderson.

"Now please, sir, if you don't mind," said Kim. "I…I think I've been raped."

By the time Crane had finished talking to Kim, he was, unfortunately, wide awake. This wasn't a dream, it was really happening. It appeared Kim had been targeted by the unknown rapist who attacked and then killed Becca Henderson. Crane phoned Derek Anderson, who was as stunned as Crane was and they agreed to meet at Kim's flat in Ascot court, near Aldershot Train Station.

Crane closed his mobile phone and stood, stretching his Sunday afternoon relaxed body, hearing the crack of bones as he rotated his neck. He needed to go and get changed into a suit, not feeling it appropriate to go out dressed in his old track suit and slippers. As he climbed the stairs he heard the merry musical box notes coming from the nursery. Looking around the door, he saw Daniel fast asleep in his cot and Tina leaning over him. As Tina followed Crane to their bedroom, he shared the news about Kim.

"Kim?" she asked. "Is she sure?"

"She must be, she's too reliable and knowledgeable to make a mistake. She can't remember much though and we think at this stage she was probably given some sort of date rape drug," Crane replied.

"But she doesn't seem the sort to get into that kind

of trouble. You know, going out with the girls to The Goose, getting drunk…" Kim frowned.

"No, you wouldn't think so. Anyway, sorry but I've got to go." Crane wanted to change the subject from Kim's plight. "Are you going to be alright?"

"Oh yes, I've got lots of housework to do to keep me busy," replied Tina.

"That's not what I meant." Crane saw the dark smudges under Tina's hollowed eyes. "Leave the housework for now," he said against his better judgement and army training. "I can do it later when I get back. Why not pop into bed and have a rest while Daniel's sleeping. You look as though you need it."

"What do you mean?" Tina was quick to bite. "Are you saying I look awful? I know you don't think I'm coping, but there's no need to be like that!"

"Like what?" Crane was genuinely confused. "I only suggested that you have a rest, for God's sake."

"It's just that you constantly pick, pick, pick," Tina responded. "Reminding me about what I haven't done, or criticising my appearance. Offering to help and then not doing it, because something comes up at work. You just don't seem to understand how I feel. I've had enough."

Tina's tirade was followed by cries from the nursery.

"Now look what you've done," she hissed. "Stop interfering."

"Oh, suit yourself," Crane shouted as he went to the bathroom and shut the door, wishing he hadn't bothered to try and be nice to Tina. He just couldn't seem to get this emotional shit right. It all seemed very straight forward to him. If Tina wasn't coping, help her. But she seemed intent on pushing away that help, which he just couldn't understand.

As he finished washing, he grabbed a towel to dry his face, scrubbing his problems at home away with the water. He'd a job to do and at the moment, that took priority over his domestic situation.

The girl sitting opposite Crane looked nothing like she did on Saturday night. Kim was huddled into a warm velour track suit, the zip of her jacket done up to her chin. Her feet were encased in socks stuffed into slippers and her hands thrust into the arms of her top. Not one piece of flesh was on view, apart from her ravaged face and even that was covered by her long blonde hair when she looked down, which was often. She was sitting on a large comfortable yellow fabric settee, under the window of her modern one bedroom rented flat. Like most young people in Aldershot, she rented what she couldn't afford to buy. The high deposits required by the banks were beyond the reach of most of them, even if they could afford to repay a large mortgage.

The purpose built blocks were situated next to Aldershot Railway Station and popular with those commuting to London. Kim had a flat at the back of the development, facing the railway tracks. Crane and Anderson were sitting opposite Kim and their conversation was occasionally interrupted by trains passing under the window, which Kim had left open.

Kim had just told them what happened. After Crane and Anderson left The Goose last night, she was approached by a tall, dark-haired young man. Making conversation, they realised they had something in common, both of them being in the army. The young man said his name was Steve and he offered to buy her a drink. She didn't really want anymore alcohol, but was persuaded have a glass of red wine.

"After that, things are pretty blurred, sir," Kim said. "I remember feeling dizzy and disorientated after I'd drunk about half the wine and that's about it. The next thing I knew, I woke up back here, on the bed. At first I didn't know where I was, but figured I must be at home, because the beads from the quilt on my bed were digging into my face. I tried to sit up, but my body felt heavy and sore and my head was pounding. Eventually I managed to roll off the bed and using the furniture to support me, I stood up. At that point the room started to spin and I felt drunk, like I did last night. I staggered to the bathroom and that's when I realised there was something more than a bad headache wrong with me. It took me quite a while to change my clothes because I kept going dizzy and after that I telephoned you."

"Sorry to ask, Kim, but where are the clothes you wore last night?"

"I've bagged them, sir. They're in an evidence pouch by the door."

Crane wondered if there were any other young women in Aldershot who kept evidence pouches in their flat and tried not to smile at the thought of Kim being so efficient that she had such items handy, just in case. Unfortunately that 'just in case' moment has arrived.

"Um, have you washed?" Crane was finding it hard to ask Kim intimate questions and he couldn't meet her eyes, preferring instead to look around the bright room, noting the contemporary furniture and the neatness.

"Of course not, sir, I've followed rape procedure. It's just that I felt so cold and needed to put on something warm. I hope I've not destroyed any evidence," Kim shivered and looked down.

"Don't worry, Kim, I'm sure you haven't," Anderson interjected. "Now, if you don't mind going with the WPC here, she'll look after you and take you to the Rape Suite at the Police Station."

Crane watched as Kim tentatively got off the settee, her knees buckling as she stood. The WPC moved in and held Kim up and together they shuffled out of the flat.

"Right, Derek," Crane was all business, falling back on his training so as not to become too emotional. He couldn't, he had a job to do. Kim's case was definitely too close for comfort. "We better get out of here as well and let forensics do their job. Thank God she wasn't killed, eh?"

"Yes. Why was that do you think?" asked Anderson.

"Fuck knows," said Crane fingering the scar under his short beard. "At the moment I'm more concerned about Kim. I'll give some thought to your question later."

Chapter 9

Crane had every right to be concerned about Kim, who was sitting quietly in the Rape Suite at Aldershot Police Station. She was silent, but not still, as she was trembling uncontrollably. Looking around the room, Kim thought the term 'suite' was somewhat erroneous. It seemed to consist of a completely plain room with a couple of armchairs and a small table in it. The cream chairs, one of which she was sitting in, faded into the cream coloured carpet and left Kim feeling that she had inexplicably landed in a vat of vanilla ice-cream. She guessed it would be difficult to know what posters or pictures to put on the beige coloured walls. You couldn't exactly put up posters extolling, 'Don't talk to strangers' or 'Don't leave your drink unattended' or even one about 'The perils of date rape drugs'. The thoughts managed to make Kim smile at the irony.

Her companion, the WPC who had led her away from her flat, was sat in the other armchair, asking her questions. Kim was trying hard to concentrate and answer them, but in her head she was screaming, *'leave me alone'*. She'd no idea what the WPC's name was. She had been told it, but just couldn't recall it. Just like she couldn't recall what had happened. She just remembered the shock of waking up and finding she had been attacked. Her head was woolly and sore, she guessed from the drug that must have been slipped into that bloody glass of wine.

'I'm sorry, Kim," the woman was saying, "but I just need to ask a few more questions, before the doctor does a physical examination. Is that okay?"

Kim nodded her agreement, finding it hard to speak over the screaming in her head.

"Firstly, I need you to understand that the doctor is needed to prove that sexual intercourse took place, to corroborate your evidence, should the case go to court."

"Go to court, of course it's going to go to bloody court, why wouldn't it?" Kim raised her voice over the noise in her head. "They're going to catch him. Sgt Major Crane and DI Anderson, I mean. They're going to catch him. I know they are. They must!"

"Please try and keep calm, Kim. I didn't mean to upset you. A court case is something we'll talk about another day. Okay?"

Kim nodded her agreement and sank further into her track suit top.

"Have you washed since you woke up this afternoon?"

"No." Kim emphasised the point with several shakes of her head.

"How about brushed your teeth?"

Again Kim shook her head.

"Have you had a cigarette?"

"No, I don't smoke."

Kim wondered when the woman was going to stop asking her bloody stupid questions.

"Have you eaten or drunk anything?"

Kim shook her head to indicate no, feeling like her brain was rattling around her skull as she moved it. The headache she'd had when she'd woken up was getting worse, not better and she desperately wanted to take something for it. But they won't let her. She also needed to soak in a long hot bath or take a long hot shower. Either would do, just so long as she could clean all this filth from her. Then she'd have to bag up this track suit, she supposed and give it to the police. Not that she wanted to see it or wear it ever again.

"Thanks for putting your clothes to one side, Kim. That will have helped our forensic team a lot. But I need to know, did you clear up anything from your flat?"

"What do you mean?" Kim whispered as the pain became a tight band around her head.

"Did you tidy up? Wash up any cups or glasses?"

"Oh, right. No, the only thing I did was to change my clothes. I had to get the filthy disgusting things off me." Kim started rubbing her arms as though trying to scrub her skin clean.

There was a knock on the door, interrupting the interview. Kim looked up and saw a policeman put his head round the door and nod to the WPC.

"Right, Kim, that's enough questions, the doctor is ready for you now."

As Kim was led into the room next door, she felt as though she was walking through water. It was an effort to push each leg through the swirling mass and she was glad of the support of the WPC.

As Kim climbed up and lay on the examination bed, the WPC turned to leave.

"No! Please stay," Kim's hand flopped around like a

fish out of water, trying to grasp the woman's hand. "Can she?" she implored.

At a nod from the doctor, the WPC clasped Kim's hand in both of hers. Kim gave her a watery smile, closed her eyes and tried to detach her mind from what the doctor was doing to her body. It must be happening to someone else. It couldn't possibly be her, lying there, being prodded and poked, scraped and photographed. It was all a big mistake. She wasn't the type of girl to get herself raped. She was a sergeant in the British Army, for God's sake, not some under dressed, over made-up, tart.

"Right Kim, up you get."

"Sorry?" The WPC's words had brought her back to reality.

"You can get up now, the doctor has finished."

Kim struggled off the bed and was handed an all in one paper jump suit.

"Can you just pop your track suit in this bag, please Kim and put this on."

As Kim did as she was asked, the WPC prattled on.

"We're going to go back next door in a minute where I'll take your statement. Don't worry about having to write it down yourself; I can do it for you."

Kim thought that was a very good idea as her hands were trembling too much to do any writing.

"It's very important that you don't leave anything out. However embarrassing or upsetting it maybe," the WPC continued.

"How can I leave anything out, when I can't remember what happened?" Kim asked as she zipped up the jumpsuit.

"Sorry, that's one of my standard phrases. I should have been more careful. But you've got a good point there about what you can and can't remember. Don't try and imagine what might have happened. Include how much you had to drink in the pub, and if you had any drinks before you left home."

"I do know about statements, thank you," Kim said as she dropped her track suit into the bag the WPC was holding open. "I am in the Military Police."

The thought of being in the army seemed to help, giving Kim the strength to stand up straight and walk unaided back into the interview room.

Chapter 10

Crane and Anderson sat disconsolately in the DI's office in Aldershot Police Station. The Monday morning blues had never seemed more appropriate. Crane kept wondering if the attack wouldn't have happened if he'd gone over to talk to Kim. If the lad really was in the army, perhaps seeing Crane and Anderson would have put him off approaching her. But that was assuming he was in the bar at the same time as them, of course.

Added to that, Crane's guilty hot pin was poking him yet again. It was late in the evening when he'd returned home yesterday. He was off again, as usual, just before 08:00 hours this morning, needing to catch up on some paperwork before he met Anderson. He was still fearful about Tina being able to cope. At the moment he wanted to be at home as often as he could to help her, but as usual, work kept getting in the way.

Shrugging away his worries, he said, "Alright, Derek, let's go over this lot one more time, starting with Blond Streak from Saturday night."

"Blond streak?" Anderson laughed for the first time that morning, spluttering over the mouthful of tea he'd been drinking. "I suppose you mean the lad Simon?"

Smiling in response, Crane admitted, "Yes, that's him. Sorry, can't get past his hair."

"Yes, well, the description he gave loosely fits that given by Becca Henderson's girlfriend. They both describe the attacker as tallish, pale skin with blond hair. Simon said he didn't remember ever seeing the lad in The Goose before that night. After what happened on Sunday afternoon, I called round to see Simon on my way home, this time with a picture of Kim. Simon said he remembered her as well. Apparently Kim stood out because she seemed quiet most of the night, not joining in too much with her friends. He described her as acting 'a bit cold and stuck up'."

"That sounds like Kim," Crane smiled. "I often wonder if she ever manages to relax. She's always so focused on her career. I can see how she would come over as detached and different from the rest of the girls."

"It's the description of the bloke Kim was with that's bothering me, though," Anderson confessed, picking up Simon's statement. "He said she was with a tallish dark-haired chap, again someone he doesn't remember seeing in the pub before."

"That ties in with Kim's statement as well," Crane said. "How come the descriptions of the rapist are so inconsistent? He was firstly blond-haired and then dark."

"Buggered if I know," grumbled Anderson. "Kim's statement isn't reliable as she was under the influence of Rohypnol. At least that's what the Doctor thinks she was given until we get the toxicology results. Come to think of it, Becca's girlfriend isn't a reliable witness as she was pretty drunk at the time."

"Hmm, but Simon wasn't drunk, nor under the influence of drugs."

"Maybe he's got it wrong."

"Let's hope so. Mind you, if he was wrong we're dealing with a serial rapist. If he's right, we're dealing with two rapists."

"It doesn't really matter either way though, does it, Crane? At the moment we've got no bloody forensic evidence to tie anybody to either incident."

Anderson pushed away his cup of tea in disgust and Crane fiddled with his scar. As there was not really much more to say, Crane left, returning to Provost Barracks to see his Officer Commanding, Captain Edwards.

Crane relayed their unfortunate lack of progress to the Captain. After taking the anticipated bollocking on the chin, Crane left the office and clattered downstairs to find Billy.

"Billy," he called as he passed his young sergeant's desk. "My office, now! Bring all the information from the computer searches and don't forget my coffee."

Crane was still angry from the derogatory remarks settled firmly on his shoulders by Captain Edwards. "You were there on Saturday night, how come you didn't spot anything?" was one of the worst. "Get out of my office and get a result," was the final shouted order.

As Billy settled himself, Crane asked, "How's Kim, sir? Bloody nasty that. But who'd have thought our Kim could actually let her hair down in the first place?"

"I spoke to her this morning. She's very shaken, as you can imagine." Crane was slumped in his chair, blowing on the fresh mug of coffee Billy had brought with him.

"So what did she look like, boss?" Billy leaned forward. "You know, all done up. Is she a bit of a looker?"

"For God's sake Billy, this is Sgt Weston you're talking about, not some tart from your local pub."

Crane banged his mug down on the desk, nearly spilling the contents all over his files.

"But she must have been up for it, boss, to go out all dressed up with a crowd of giggling girls, sat in The Goose. It's renowned that place. I've been there a few times myself to see what's on offer."

"Shut the fuck up, Billy and let's get on with the job of finding her attacker."

"Sorry, sir," Billy looks suitably contrite.

"I should bloody well think so. Now, what did the searches I requested last week throw up?"

Crane pushed his coffee and some files out of the way, to clear a space on his desk.

"Well, sir, here's the print out."

Billy lifted a mountain of paper from the floor and it hit Crane's desk with an ominous thud. There was a piece of paper sticking out of it and Billy used this to separate the print out into two piles.

"This left hand pile is soldiers on Aldershot Garrison who fit the dark-haired description," he said. "The one on the right I did this morning, it's of soldiers who fit the blond-haired description."

"Shit," Crane shook his head and frowned.

"Exactly, boss. Just to make sure the search was thorough, I looked for my name and there I am nearly at the end of the list, my surname being Williams."

"I'm well aware of your surname, Billy."

"Yes, sir, sorry, sir."

"Have you any other gems of information for me?"

"Not really, other than we'd tie up all of SIB and the RMP trying to interview this lot."

"Yes, you're right," sighed Crane. "How about narrowing both searches to those soldiers who were off-duty that night and take out officers and higher ranks. I reckon our suspect was probably no higher than Lance Corporal, mostly because of his age. Do that for both the dark-haired and blond-haired searches and don't forget the dates are different."

"Of course not, sir, what do you take me for?"

"A fool when it comes to computers."

Crane had obviously hit a nerve, as Billy's face suffused with colour.

"Let me have the results as soon as you can."

"Of course, sir, probably tomorrow morning."

"Very well. Oh, while Kim's out of the office, you'll just have to use Sally to help out with any admin tasks. It's been approved by Captain Edwards. Sally may not be too happy about it though, it's doubling her work load, so tread carefully and only use her when absolutely necessary. You'll also have to help with the more routine tasks, so you better get started on the incident boards while the computer's doing its thing with the searches. Dismissed."

Crane needed to see Staff Sgt Jones of the Royal Military Police. But before he walked the short distance to Jones' office, he diverted to the car park where he had a quick cigarette. As he smoked he thought about Billy's observations about Kim and the girls in general who frequent The Goose. He could see Billy's point of view, one that he held himself, if he was perfectly honest, especially after his experience that first Saturday

53

night in the town centre. But the generic description of the girls who frequent The Goose, just didn't fit Kim. From what Crane could remember, her clothes were similar to those the other girls were wearing, but there was no stomach on show, no tits thrust upward, no acres of thigh on display. So why was she chosen? Why didn't the rapist pick on some one less subtle? For the moment, Crane couldn't make head or tail of it all. But he would, given time. It was his personal promise to Kim.

Chapter 11

Staff Sergeant Jones wasn't as helpful as Billy, but then he was more of an equal to Crane than Billy was. "You want me to what?" was his reaction to Crane's demand, rather than request.

"Interview the RMPs who were out in Aldershot town centre the last two Saturday nights. See if they remember seeing a tallish, dark-haired squaddie or a tallish blond-haired squaddie helping an intoxicated girl," Crane repeated his request.

"Helping her do what exactly?" Jones shook his shaven head. He was another man who was going bald and had decided to hide the fact by taking off his remaining hair. Being Royal Military Police and not SIB, Jones was dressed in uniform, the buttons of his tunic glinting in the overhead fluorescent lights. His cap was placed carefully on top of a filing cabinet and his desk was lined with baskets of paper, in the otherwise small empty office.

"I don't know, Jones. Perhaps helping her into a car, into a taxi or just walking along the road. Someone somewhere must have seen Becca Henderson or Kim being led away by their attacker. Or attackers."

"Well which is it, one attacker or two?"

"I wish I bloody knew, Staff. For the moment, let's treat it as two different men."

The scar on Crane's face got yet more attention.

"Look, Crane, I'll do what I can, but I've not got much to go on here. Any chance of a better description or an artist's impression?"

Jones jotted down a couple of notes on his pad.

"How the hell am I supposed to get one of those, Jones? Becca is dead and Kim remembers very little due to the drug. We'll just have to work with what we've got, which is pictures of the two girls."

Crane's mobile interrupted their conversation.

"Hang on," he asked Jones, fishing it out of his pocket. He glanced at the caller ID before accepting the call. After agreeing with the caller and closing the phone, Crane said, "Right, Staff, got to go. Billy needs me. Do what you can, eh?"

"Of course, but remember it's as bad as looking for a needle in a haystack. Don't hold your breath for any results."

"Any more clichés for me?" Crane laughed and ducked as Jones sent a ball of paper flying his way.

The next meeting Crane attended was a more sombre affair. The call to Crane's mobile was Billy saying the young soldier who was raped had agreed to a meeting. But it had to be now and at the venue of his choice.

The place he had picked was the cafeteria in the local Tesco supermarket. Crane pulled up in the car park, got out of the car and rummaged around in the boot. Satisfied with his selection he quickly took off his jacket, white short sleeved shirt and tie, replacing them with a casual black high necked jumper and baseball cap. He couldn't do anything about his trousers, or his beard, but took a pair of glasses from the glove box, which had plain glass lenses.

As he entered the cafeteria, he saw Billy and another man sitting in a corner of the teaming cafe. It seemed the victim thought there was safety in numbers. The idea being to blend into the background, Crane supposed, a form of camouflage. He stood in the queue of the self service café, with a number of Aldershot's finest. Women were calling to each other over the general hubbub. Those saving a table shouted their orders to those who were waiting in line. Children whined for the last sticky bun, favourite chocolate bar or large bag of crisps, whose mothers bought the items just to shut the kids up.

At last Crane got to Billy's table, putting his cup of coffee down and staring at it with distaste. The weak greasy brew looked particularly unappetising. Lifting his head he nodded to Billy and then looked at the victim. He saw a young soldier who looked much like any other. The lad's hair was cut very close to his head, so he looks bald at first glance. His physique was lean and fit and he didn't appear to have any distinguishing marks that Crane could see. In any event, there were no tattoos on his arms, which were poking out of a short sleeved tee-shirt.

The only difference separating him from any other squaddie was his eyes. Haunted was the description that sprang to Crane's mind. Crane also noticed that he was fiddling with his plastic beaker of cold drink. Turning it round and round and frequently glancing down at it.

"Seb, this was the man I was telling you about," Billy said, obviously being careful not to use military language, so Crane followed suit.

"Pleased to meet you," Crane said, but stopped short of offering his hand to shake, nodding his head instead. Crane wasn't prepared to suppress military conventions to that extent.

Turner didn't speak, just nodded back at Crane.

"I wonder if you could reassure Seb about our discretion, um, when it comes to, um… matters like this," Billy finally spat out, the tips of his ears going pink.

"Sure."

Crane relaxed back in his chair, not wanting to give other customers the impression that some sort of secret meeting was going on. Even though that's what it really was.

"If you decide you want our help, I can assure you that anything you say will be completely confidential, until such a time as we have enough evidence to, um," Crane wanted to say 'press charges' but settled for, "deal with it. Only then will any action be taken and even then, not without your consent. At no time will your identity be public knowledge, although it may be better in the long run to transfer you into another, um," Crane looked around to make sure no one was obviously listening to their conversation and finished with "sector," in lieu of Regiment.

Keeping up the pretence of a casual meeting between friends, Crane lent forward and lifted his coffee to his lips and managed to take a sip of the weak cup of mostly hot water without grimacing. He wondered if Turner was going to be brave enough to go through with this as at the words 'deal with it', what little colour he had in his face, drained away.

"We only want to help, Seb," Billy said, playing with his own plastic beaker. "Don't let the bastard get away with it," he hissed. "Try and fight back."

Billy's words had such an impact that Turner's Adam's apple bobbed up and down several times before he crushed his empty drinks beaker with more force than necessary, stood and hurried out of the cafeteria.

Taking their time, Crane and Billy cleared the table and left the cafe, not saying anything until they were standing by Crane's car.

"That went well then," said Crane.

A letter to Sgt Major Crane

Sir,

I wanted to thank you for taking the time to come and meet me yesterday. I feel ashamed now that I didn't even have the decency to speak to you. Not one word. Instead I turned tail and ran way.

I've been thinking about that a lot, my running away. Not just physically from you, but running away from my problems, not being able to turn and face them. Turn and face the bastard who has ruined my life. It's as though I'm in limbo. Torn in two. Half man, half wimp. Half soldier, half coward. I'm just so bloody confused and so ashamed.

I think I need to be more like 'the mouse who roared'. You know the kid's book where a mouse is so timid and frightened of everyone. But he discovers that he can roar like a lion and tricks everyone into thinking he is this great big angry beast that all the animals are frightened of. An outward persona of the king of the jungle, but inside, still a small trembling mouse.

So give me just a bit more time then I'll slip on my lion's costume and be ready. Ready to roar at the top of my voice, ready to make the ground shake under my violator's feet, ready to see him quake in fear when he meets me face to face in court.

In time.

Chapter 12

Crane suddenly found the red flock wallpaper in Kim's parents' house rather interesting. As he minutely examined the repeat pattern, Kim's sobs subsided and he could hear her trying to control her breathing, every now and then hitching over a held back sob.

"I'm sorry, sir," she said.

Crane looked at her, sitting on the black settee, eyes, nose and mouth red and swollen from her emotional outburst, as though garish, outlandish makeup had been applied with a less than steady hand. A WPC was sitting next to her, holding a box of tissues. Crane and Anderson were sitting in separate armchairs, facing Kim.

"Sorry? Whatever for, Kim?" he asked.

"For all of this," she spread her arms, palms upward. "I should be at the Garrison, on duty, running the office for you and Billy, not sat here snivelling on the settee. It's my fault. Everything's my fault."

Crane's mouth opened and then closed again. He just didn't have the words, didn't know what to say to this fine young soldier who was falling apart in front of him.

Derek Anderson stepped in and saved him, leaning forward and saying, "Of course it's not your fault, Kim. It's the fault of that, that, monster," Anderson spat out the last word. "Look, if you think you can manage it, the best way to help us is by trying to remember what he looked like. We need a description. We've got nothing."

"I'll tell you what," the WPC said, "if I stay here and hold your hand, could you just close your eyes and think back to Saturday night."

"Okay, I'll try,"

Kim grabbed the WPC's hand, her breathing becoming slower as her body went limp and she relaxed back against the cushions.

"What's the first thing you remember?" the WPC asked.

"Um, being in The Goose."

"What was it like in there?"

"Busy, hot, noisy."

"Can you remember being approached by him?"

Crane noticed Kim flinch, but then she took a deep breath and continued.

"Um, yes, I noticed him up at the bar. He caught my eye but I turned and looked at one of the girls at my table. I wasn't really interested in finding a boyfriend, so I ignored him. When I looked back at the bar, he'd gone. But then he seemed to come out of nowhere and the next thing I knew he was sitting next to me."

"That's really good, Kim. Can you describe him?"

But Kim appeared not to have heard the question. In fact she seemed not to be hearing or seeing anything. Nothing here in the room at least. Crane watched in horror as she pressed back into the settee, her legs scrabbling at the floor. Her hand pulled free from the

WPC and she started to beat the air in front of her, fighting an invisible opponent.

"What the hell!" Crane jumped to his feet. "What's wrong with her?" he demanded.

"I think she's having a flashback, sir. We'll just have to wait until she comes out of it."

Just as the WPC finished speaking, Kim screamed, arching her back, then collapsed back onto the settee, subsiding into sobs.

"It's alright, Kim, shush," the WPC crooned, smoothing down Kim's hair, in an effort to calm her down.

"Water, sir?" The WPC asked Crane.

"No thanks," he said. "Oh, you mean get some for Kim?" Crane moved towards the kitchen as the WPC nodded.

When he returned, with his dignity more or less intact after that blunder, Kim had pulled her legs up onto the settee and was curled into the policewoman's side. She was talking softly to her. Crane strained to hear, staying where he was, not wanting to break the bond forming between the two women.

"Dark, I remember dark."

"Hair or skin?" asked the WPC.

"His skin. He wasn't black, just tanned if you like, foreign sort of, not pale white anyway."

"What about his hair?"

"It, it, was also dark."

"What about a beard?"

Kim shook her head in denial.

"Did he have a goatee? How about those razor sharp lines some of the lads sport, you know a bit like the celebrities have."

"No, no facial hair. Clean shaven."

"You're doing really well, Kim. Can you remember if he had any tattoos or marks on his hands or arms?" The WPC was still talking softly, still holding Kim close to her.

"No - I can't remember any more. No more questions, please. I just want to be left alone now. Sorry," Kim sniffed back a sob.

"No need to be sorry, Kim. It's not your fault. You might remember more in time. Here, take this water," Crane said and held out the glass to her.

But Kim didn't reach for the water, looking instead at the WPC in horror. "You mean I'm going to have more of those, those, what did you call them, flashbacks?"

"Probably, maybe, who knows? Everyone is different. Everyone's healing process is different. I know it's painful and horrific, but if you do have any more and remember anything else, please let us know."

Kim mutely looked at the WPC, her eyes filling with tears once again, but she managed a small nod.

Crane cleared his throat and handed the WPC the glass of water he was still holding, as he didn't know what else to do with it. He was very glad she was there. He'd have made a right mess of it without her help. This wasn't the same as interviewing angry squaddies, or even jumped up officers. This was something completely outside of his experience, leaving him feeling bewildered and exhausted. He hoped he wouldn't have to go through it again in the future with any more girls. He'd better make sure of that - by catching the bastard.

Chapter 13

Crane's eyes were hurting, so he rubbed them and once again returned to the computer print out in front of him.

"I see what you mean, Billy. This is a complete bloody nightmare. There are still hundreds of either blond-haired or dark-haired soldiers off duty the previous two Saturdays."

Billy stood and moved away from his place opposite Crane at the conference table. They had moved from Crane's office so they had room to spread out the pieces of paper from the computer searches.

"Sorry, boss, even though I changed the search parameters as you suggested, there are still too many lads on the list."

Crane also stood and prowled, moving over to the two incident boards, one for the rape and murder of Becca Henderson and one for Kim's rape. Both boards had pictures of the victims on, but no photos of possible perpetrators. Not even any names that needed investigating.

"This is pointless. I'm going to have to speak to DI Anderson, see if he's got anything more that may help us. Stop going through these, Billy, it's a waste of time. Let's look at the records for the blokes in Private

Turner's Company. We may as well concentrate on his rape case for now. Put this lot away," Crane gestured to the table, "and get out the others, while I have a ciggie."

Banging his way out of the office, Crane paced around the car park, drawing deeply on his cigarette. This should be his office. He did his best thinking in the car park, at times accompanied by Staff Sergeant Jones. Today, in early October, the weather was surprisingly calm. The whole of the summer had been dominated by rains and floods, so fine, sunny, autumn days were a bonus.

Over the weekend, because of the good weather, he and Tina had taken Daniel out for walks in his pushchair. Crane was glad to get away from the claustrophobic house that seemed to be totally focused on the baby. Also Crane's predilection for tidiness was putting Tina under some strain. He wished she'd be more diligent about putting things away once they had been used. She still left the nursery in a bloody mess, despite his system, shelves and cupboards. If he had to tidy the place up one more time, he thought he'd scream.

He pulled out his mobile, going to the camera function and looking at the images he had of Daniel. As he smiled at the antics of his young son, he acknowledged that things were gradually getting better at home. Thank God for Jean Anderson. Tina was keeping up the bottle routine with Daniel and it had had the calming effect Crane was hoping for. Tina was less tired, Daniel wasn't hungry and as a result Crane was happier.

Realising that none of this introspection was helping with the two rape cases on his books, Crane threw away the butt of his cigarette and went to see what Billy had.

Billy was just finishing printing off the records as Crane walked back in to the office, so he collected a cup of coffee and then returned to the conference table. As he sat down, Billy walked up and plonked down a small stack of paper on the table.

"This looks a bit more manageable."

"Yes, sir. These are the records of all corporals and lance corporals in A Company."

"Right then, let's get started."

As they reviewed the records, Crane was particularly looking for anyone that had previous incidents of anger, violence or bullying. He thought that just maybe this rape was being perpetrated by a hot head, someone who loved throwing his weight around and who enjoyed controlling the men under his command. If that was the case, there should be hints about it from any brushes with the Military Police, or alluded to in Confidential Reports.

As he sorted through the papers, Crane realised there was a big mix of ethnic backgrounds in the lads, no doubt part of the army recruitment campaigns, ensuring they met the Government targets on open recruitment. Also, officers and sergeants in each company would have paid particular mind to ethnicity when promoting through the ranks. Making sure everyone had the same promotional opportunities, leaving no room for any possible racial or victimisation cases.

Studying the photographs, Crane found there were a number of them who had dark hair and darkish skin. Some of Pakistani or Indian descent, others clearly coming from mixed marriages and others who only had a hint of their original ethnicity, which had been watered down with each generation. He put these to one side.

"Billy," he said, lifting his head from the records.

"Boss?"

"Sort through your pile of records and pull out the ones who are dark-haired and darker skinned, would you?"

"Okay, boss, but why?"

"Because Kim said she thought her attacker had olive sort of skin, so just get me the records."

Billy shuffled papers for a few minutes, while Crane tapped his pen on the table and then fingered his scar.

"Here you are, sir," Billy handed the records over.

"About time," Crane grumbled and spread the three records from Billy across his side of the table, adding them to the five from his pile. Studying the pictures closely he immediately discarded four of them.

Handing the remainder to Billy he said, "Look up these four on the computer. See if any of them were off-duty last Saturday night."

"Yes, boss."

Billy looked at Crane as if to say something else but Crane's glare stopped him and he walked across the office to his desk. After a few clicks and clacks and 'bloody hell's' Billy was back.

"Right, sir. These two were off-duty on Saturday night, Lance Corporals Whadi and Johnson." He handed the two records to Crane. "Lance Corporal Hicks was on exercise," Billy continued, then stopped speaking, no doubt realising he was talking to Crane's back.

"Sir?"

"I'll be with DI Anderson if anyone wants me," Crane called over his shoulder as he left the SIB office clutching the two files.

"So, what do you think, Derek?"

Crane was pacing up and down Anderson's office in Aldershot Police Station. Or more like going round in circles. There was hardly any clear floor space in the office, as papers, files and books littered Anderson's desk, cabinets and visitor chairs.

"It's a bit bloody tenuous, Crane. Total speculation, that's what I think."

"Well, no it isn't, not really, Derek." Crane was stung by Anderson's words. "If you think about it, Kim said she was chatted up by a soldier, right?"

"Right."

"And he had dark hair and darkish skin."

"Right again."

"So, it makes sense to look at dark-haired, dark-skinned soldiers that were off-duty on Saturday night."

"I know that, Crane, but you pulled hundreds of dark-haired blokes off the computer. You've just told me that yourself. What makes these two soldiers any different? Why do they stand out? Just because you weeded them out whilst investigating another rape case, doesn't mean to say they had anything to do with Kim's attack. As I said, it's pure speculation."

"Alright, Derek, but isn't that what we do at the start of a case, speculate? Anyway, we've got nothing else to go on, so we may as well at least talk to Kim and show her the photos. I am using some filters, you know. There were a number of lads who were clearly too dark-skinned to fit the frame and one or two even had designer stubble, for Christ's sake. At least I've picked the only two who match her description."

"Oh, very well, I might as well give in," Anderson groaned. "If I don't, you'll not leave it alone. I know you too well. Let me ring the WPC, see if she's free and if she is we'll all go over and see Kim. I'm only doing this interview with someone there who can give Kim emotional support, as showing her photographs of possible suspects could send her over the edge again. As it did the last time we asked her some questions."

Chapter 14

To Crane's disappointment Kim was pretty much in the same state as she was a few days ago. Her eyes were sad and she was still wearing clothes that covered her from head to foot. Her long blond hair was hanging dull and lifeless around her shoulders. The WPC was talking quietly to her, asking her how she was feeling today, whispering words of encouragement, sympathy and support.

Crane was still standing and took a moment to look around Kim's family home. The home she had been forced to return to, because she felt her own flat had been contaminated. Crane doubted she would ever return to it, which was a shame as it was a lovely property that Kim had made her own. Perhaps she would move onto the Garrison when she felt stronger, he thought, but for now she was staying with her parents. Warm and comforting were words that sprung to mind to describe their home. The old furniture was glowing, there was what appeared to be a television cabinet in the corner and the room was topped off with pretty matching curtains and cushions. Dotted around were several pictures of Kim from her army career. The three that caught Crane's eyes were her passing out parade, Kim in the middle of a laughing crowd of fellow soldiers and Kim displaying her sergeant's stripes with pride.

He dragged his eyes from the photos and looked at the WPC, raising his eyebrows, wanting to know if they could get on with it. She nodded her agreement to Crane's unspoken question and stood up so that Crane and Anderson could move to either side of Kim on the settee.

"We just want you to look at some photos, please, Kim," said Anderson.

Kim turned to look, not at Anderson, but at Crane and he saw the fear in her eyes.

"Only if you're up to it," Crane said, not wanting to put pressure on Kim, but at the same time not really meaning it, as he needed to see her reaction to the photos.

"It's alright, sir, I don't mind," she replied, but she couldn't keep eye contact with either man for long and soon dropped her gaze to her lap.

Crane got several pictures out of his pocket. "We wondered, well I did," Crane quickly added after a glare from Anderson, "if either of these men look familiar."

He put the pictures on Kim's lap.

Kim picked them up, looking at each one in turn.

"Take your time, Kim, there's no rush," Anderson said as Kim repeatedly looked though them.

"I don't know," she said so quietly, Crane had to strain to hear her. "If anything, it's this one," she passed a photo to Crane. "He looks familiar, but I can't say where from. I just know I've seen him before."

A shudder passed through Kim's body.

"Thanks, Kim, that's really helpful," said Anderson

lifting his arm as though to put it around Kim, but putting it up to his head instead, trying to flatten what was left of his wispy gray hair.

Crane retrieved the other photos from Kim and moved from the settee, taking down one of her army pictures.

"I was looking at this when we came in," he said, showing it to her. "When was this taken? About a year ago?"

Kim nodded.

"It's a brilliant photo, don't you think, Derek?"

Anderson nodded his agreement.

"I bet you felt really proud then, didn't you Kim?"

"Yes, sir," Kim replied, lifting her head just a little.

"It's no mean feat that, you know, getting your sergeant's stripes. You got them just before you transferred to SIB, didn't you?"

"Yes, sir," Kim said, this time looking up at Crane.

"Bloody good achievement that. Not many make the grade, you know, men or women. You have to be something special to get into SIB."

"You think so, sir?"

"I know so, Kim," Crane squatted down in front of her. "You are a fine soldier, Kim. One of the best and don't *ever* forget that."

"No, sir, thank you, sir," Kim's voice was gaining strength and she was looking Crane in the eye.

"Good, so remember, don't let the bastards grind you down. You're better than that, worth more than that, understood?"

At those words, Kim smiled, "Understood, sir, thank you."

Crane's little pep talk was interrupted by a tap on the living room door and he got up as her mother came in.

"Sorry to bother you all, but this has just arrived for Kim," she said, holding out a slim box. The WPC moved to take it from Mrs Weston and passed the box onto Kim.

As Anderson and Crane stood around awkwardly, not knowing if they should leave, Kim unwrapped the box. In it was a single red rose with a small card nestling in the petals. She picked up the card and read it.

"Who's it from, Kim?" the WPC asked.

But all Kim could do was shake her head saying, "No, no, get it off me, get it away from me!"

The box and card went flying and Kim lifted her feet off the floor pushing backwards on the settee, as though in fear of a mouse or spider on the floor. She was clearly desperate to get as far away as possible from the flower. With some trepidation Crane picked up the card from the floor and read it:

I enjoyed our date on Saturday night.
I hope you did too.

As he silently passed it to Anderson, Kim started screaming.

Chapter 15

Crane and Anderson immediately moved to the living room door.

"When did this arrive?" Crane asked Kim's mother, having to raise his voice over Kim's screams.

"Just now," Mrs Weston looked bewildered by the havoc she had caused.

"Was it a delivery?" Anderson asked.

Kim's mother nodded in reply.

As Crane and Anderson burst out of the front door, a man was just getting into the driver's side of a plain white van, parked on the opposite side of the street. Anderson rushed across the road, grabbed him and pulled him from the vehicle before the man could close the door.

"Oy, what are you doing?" the man shouted.

"Shut the fuck up," Anderson said, pushing his ID in the man's bespectacled face, simultaneously pushing him up against the side of his van. "Police."

"This is police brutality," he spat at Anderson.

"How about a bit of army brutality?"

Crane pushed Anderson out of the way and slammed into the man, putting his hand on his throat and squeezing.

"Who the hell are you and why did you just make a delivery here?"

Unfortunately Crane and Anderson couldn't understand the choked reply, so Crane loosened his grip on the man's throat, just a bit.

"Some bloke asked me to do it."

"Some bloke? What bloke?" Anderson demanded.

"I don't know, he gave me a tenner," the man managed to gasp out, despite Crane's grip.

"Let go of his throat, Crane."

"But…"

"I said let go. We'll take him down to the station and see what we can get out of him. It's not the rapist. Look at him. He doesn't fit the description."

Crane had to agree, the man being squat and dumpy and at least fifty years old, so Crane took his hand from the man's throat. But making sure he still had a hold on the man, Crane took the driver's arm with one hand and his wrist with the other, twisting his arm so that if he moved he would break it. Anderson made his phone call and within a few minutes a police car arrived.

"What about my van?" the driver protested, as he was unceremoniously pushed into the back of the police car.

"You can get it later after I've finished with you at the station." Slamming the door Anderson tapped twice on the roof and stayed in the middle of the road, watching the police car speed away.

A little while later Anderson and Crane watched the van driver through the two way mirror of an interview room in Aldershot Police Station.

"His name's John Smith," Anderson commented.

"You've got to be kidding me," laughed Crane. "He must get a lot of stick about pints of beer."

"Yeah, well, just now he's going to get a lot of stick off me, for delivering that flower to Kim," said Anderson.

"It was bloody bad timing. I was just trying to rally Kim round with thoughts of the army, her career and stuff." Crane put his hands around the back of his neck, trying to massage away the tightness. "Now she's back to square one. Bastard."

"Who, the attacker or the delivery man?" asked Anderson.

"Both of them."

"Come on," smiled Anderson, "let's see what we can get out of him."

As Crane and Anderson entered the room, Smith's head shot up from where he was sitting at the table, examining his filthy nails.

"Look, just leave me alone will you, I don't know anything."

"Oh, but you do, Mr Smith," said Anderson. "At least more than you think you do."

Joining Smith at the table, Anderson activated the recording system. He then identified himself and Crane, as per procedure when conducting an interview.

"So, Mr Smith," said Anderson, "who approached you and asked you to deliver the parcel?"

"Some bloke I was talking to in the pub."

"And what did this bloke look like?" asked Crane.

"Um, taller than me and slimmer than me…"

"That's not difficult," mumbled Crane under his breath.

"What?"

"Nothing. You were saying, Mr Smith."

"Yeah, well, he was tall, slim, with blondish hair."

"What were you two talking about?" asked Anderson.

"Um, just stuff, this and that."

"Could you be more specific, please, Mr Smith?"

Crane wanted to add a more sarcastic comment, but stopped himself just in time.

"Yeah, well, he was in the army, like, so he was telling me war stories and stuff." Smith leaned back in his chair, clasping his hands and resting them on his rotund stomach.

At this piece of news Anderson's eyebrows lifted and he looked at Crane.

"Did he give you specifics about his rank, or regiment?" Crane demanded.

"Don't think so and if he did I wouldn't have understood it. That army bollocks makes no sense to me."

"What did he say about the package?" Anderson steered the conversation back to the matter in hand.

"He just said he needed it delivering to his girlfriend. He couldn't do it as he was due back on the Garrison, but he really wanted her to have it today, as it was her birthday. So he wondered if I could help him out, like. I told him I could, for a fee. So he gave me a tenner and wrote down the address."

"Wrote it down?"

"That's what I just said, innit?"

"Do you still have the paper?"

"Yeah, here it is."

Smith scrabbled through his pockets, tossing a crumpled piece of paper on the desk. Crane and Anderson both looked at it, without touching it. It was a handwritten note scribbled on a piece of paper, which looked like it had been torn out of a notebook. Anderson hunted in his own pockets and came up with a pair of latex gloves and an evidence pouch. Putting on the gloves, he carefully pulled the paper straight and inserted it into the evidence pouch.

"Right, Mr Smith," Anderson was the first to break the silence. "Thanks very much for being so helpful. If you just wait here, someone will transcribe your statement and bring it back for you to sign."

As Crane and Anderson reached the door, Smith shouted after them, "You still haven't told me what this bloke's done. I've never known such a fuss over delivering a birthday present."

Crane was the one who answered. "It wasn't a birthday present. It was a psychological attack on a vulnerable young woman who had been physically assaulted."

"Right," Smith mumbled. "Sorry, I didn't know, like. I didn't mean any harm," he finished, but Crane and Anderson didn't reply and shut the door on him.

Back in his office, Anderson sat and filled out an evidence form for the piece of paper, then shouted for a PC to take it to forensics.

"Don't suppose we'll get much off it," he grumbled, fidgeting in his chair. "That bloody man's had his hands all over it and it's been crumpled and stuffed into his trouser pocket."

"Never mind, it might help with hand writing verification," mused Crane, fingering his scar.

"Yes, but that's not an exact science is it? Not like DNA. Anyway, Smith's description of Kim's attacker is way off. He reckons he's blondish and Kim said he was dark-haired."

"Yes, I did notice that," said Crane. "I wonder what the hell it means."

Chapter 16

Crane couldn't believe that he was yet again on the streets of Aldershot on a Saturday night. It was really starting to piss him off, all this work and no results. Or at least the results they had got didn't mean a bloody thing. Still, at least tonight he didn't have to worry about Tina. Jean Anderson had arranged to go over and spend the evening with her, complete with a take-away and a romantic comedy film. As he and Derek tramped from pub to pub, Crane almost wished he was at home with them, although he hated Indian food and romantic comedies. Yes, almost wished, but not quite.

A wall of noise slammed into them whenever they opened the door to a pub, giving Crane a headache. The heat inside meant Crane was constantly taking his coat on and off. If he left it on, he sweated so much he feared he was leaving puddles on the carpet. Not that anyone would notice, as most of the carpets were filthy and felt sticky underfoot. Crane expected that most of the establishments must look a right mess in daylight. After several fruitless questions at most of the pubs in and around Victoria Road, they finished up at The Goose.

"I don't know why we didn't start here in the first place," Crane grumbled to Anderson. "This was where both girls were picked up, for God's sake. It made sense to me."

"Ah, yes, but if we'd got a result here first, then you'd have pissed off, running away with the information like a Labrador with a ball, potentially missing a vital piece of information from another pub."

"But we didn't pick up any bits of information, or possible sightings, from any of the other pubs, vital or otherwise, did we?"

"Well, no, but my theory is still sound," insisted Anderson, stuffing his hands in his pockets against the cold night air.

Crane realised he was not going to win that particular argument, so he stopped moaning and approached the two bouncers on the door.

Flashing his ID he said, "Sgt Major Crane, SIB and DI Anderson, Aldershot Police. Have either of you seen these blokes before?"

"You've got to be joking, SIB and the police in one visit? Are you trying to put off our punters or what?"

"Maybe that's not a bad idea, seeing as what this bloke's done," growled Crane. "So look at the pictures."

The two men looked at Anderson, who nodded his agreement.

The first one took the pictures, holding them up to the light spilling from the open doorway behind him.

"No, sorry, mate, can't help."

"What about you?"

Crane grabbed back the photos and thrust them under the nose of the second man.

"Nah," he said without really looking.

"Try again," said Anderson, taking a couple of steps

forward to emphasis his point.

"Alright, alright."

The man looked more carefully this time, frowning over one of them.

"Hang on," he said, turning and moving just inside the door, where the light was brighter. "I reckon I've seen this one before," he handed the picture back to Crane.

"When?"

"Earlier this evening. He came in on his own, which was unusual, normally you get a few blokes arriving at the same time, on a night out with the lads, that sort of thing. That's why I noticed him."

"Has he left?" asked Anderson.

"No bloody idea, mate. I don't look at the ones leaving, only the ones coming in. That's the general idea of a bouncer, innit?"

After that piece of information, Crane went through the door to the pub, shouldering away anyone in his path.

"Crane," Anderson shouted.

Crane ignored Anderson and pushed through the crowds, quickly scanning each table. There was no point in checking the photo, the light was too bad, but he didn't need to. The man's features were burned into his brain since Kim identified him as possibly being her attacker. Working his way around the large pub Crane eventually found a familiar face, but it wasn't that of the suspected rapist.

"Billy! What the hell are you doing here? Get out, now."

As Crane walked out of the pub, with Billy scampering behind him and Anderson trying to catch them both up, he pulled out his cigarettes.

"Thank God. Bloody hell it's hot and noisy in there. Right, Billy, what are you doing here?"

"I'm off-duty, sir."

"I know that, sergeant. What precisely are you doing in The Goose?"

Crane dipped his head to light his cigarette.

"Well, sort of staking out the joint, sir."

"Staking out the joint," Anderson laughed as he joined them. "We're not in a gangster movie, Billy."

Billy had the good grace to blush before he continued.

"Well, sir, I just thought I might keep an eye out, see if I could see anyone fitting the description in that photo Kim identified. Or see any girls looking a bit worse for wear, being helped out of the pub."

"I should think that's most of them, isn't it?"

Anderson was still chuckling and watching a crowd of girls totter up the street.

"Anyway, you haven't needed me much lately, sir. You've mostly been working with the DI here, so I just thought I'd do my bit to help. You've both ruined it for me tonight, though, haven't you? Pushing me out of the door like that, like a common criminal. I left my coat behind as well and it's freezing out here."

Billy shivered dramatically as he was only dressed in a lightweight short sleeved shirt and thin trousers.

Crane wasn't about to apologise for Billy feeling left out. Instead he went on the attack.

"Well, you didn't do a very good job, because apparently one of the bouncers reckons he saw our suspect coming in tonight."

"Oh," Billy looked from Crane to Anderson and back. "Well, there were so many blokes in there," Billy pointed with his thumb over his shoulder, "it was difficult to keep tabs on who I'd looked at and who I hadn't."

"Exactly, Billy, that's why we're talking to the doormen, they're the only ones who get a good look at everyone coming in and out," said Anderson.

"Mind you, that's given me an idea," Crane said. "How good do you look in a dark overcoat and sunglasses Billy?"

Once Crane and Anderson had taken the details of the bouncer who recognised the lad in their photo and arranged for him to give a statement at Aldershot Police Station the next day, they turned to the subject of the suspect, Lance Corporal Whadi, as they walk back to their car.

"Well, I think I ought to pull him in on Monday and interview him. Better involve Billy, I suppose, as he seems to be feeling a bit left out," said Crane.

"And me," added Anderson.

"And me, what? Ah, are you feeling left out too?" Crane said in a high pitched voice.

"Alright, very funny, ha ha. I meant include me in the interview. Just tell me where and when."

"It's alright, Derek, this is army business."

"Don't give me that bollocks, Crane. We're either working this one together or we're not. If we are, I come to the interview. If we're not, you get no more special access to the investigation. Got it?"

Looking at Anderson's red face and clenched fists, Crane realised he'd made an error of judgement. The case was too important for him not to be fully involved. Otherwise, how could he avenge Kim's attack? After a few moments of staring at Anderson, he relaxed and said, "Of course you can come, Derek." But he didn't apologise. Crane didn't really do apologies.

Chapter 17

The following day, Crane's Sunday was interrupted once again. He was none too pleased when Tina answered the telephone and announced that Anderson wanted to speak to him.

Leaving the table with a last lingering look at his plate piled high with beef, Yorkshire pudding and vegetables, he went through to the hall to take Anderson's call.

"This better be good, Derek," Crane said without preamble.

"Good afternoon to you as well, Crane.

"What? Oh, right. Well, what do you want? Why aren't you relaxing in front of the television full of food and beer?"

"Because there's been another murder."

"Jesus Christ."

"Exactly, Crane, same method as Becca Henderson, raped then strangled."

"Are you at the scene now?"

"Yes, I've just arrived."

"Give me the address then and I'll meet you there."

After scribbling down the details on the pad kept by

the telephone, Crane went back into the kitchen to apologise yet again to Tina for leaving her, for the second Sunday in a row. She pretended it was okay, but Crane could see tears glinting in her eyes as she took his plate from the table and turned away from him.

"It's alright, Tom, I understand."

She turned on the taps to fill the sink with hot water.

"I'll get on with the chores while Daniel is still asleep. I won't be able to do much else once he wakes up."

"Tina, love, don't be silly. Why don't you just leave the kitchen until I get back? Finish your dinner first and then grab a rest while you can. I'll sort this lot out later."

"I can't do that, though, can I, Tom?"

Tina turned, her eyes blazing in a face as white as her tee shirt.

"You're always telling me not to leave a mess, to get a job finished before I start on the next one. Telling me to keep the house tidy and the nursery tidy, so your bloody systems work properly. God almighty! Why is it always so difficult living with a soldier? You're all the bloody same, you know. Do you know that's what the girls talk about at the mother and baby group? That their husbands have such high standards and how hard it is living up to them."

Tears were streaming down Tina's face as she pushed past him, sitting down at the kitchen table with a thump. She wiped her face with a tea towel, but the tears didn't stop.

"Tina, I'm so sorry," Crane sat next to her and held her hand. "I don't mean to criticise all the time. It's just so difficult separating the two halves of my life. The army life and our home life. Come on, you know what they say - old habits die hard!"

Crane forced a laugh, but Tina didn't respond to his cajoling. But for once Crane didn't give up.

"Come on, love, go through to the other room. Put your feet up on the settee and watch an old Agatha Christie film, or something. I'll sort the kitchen out now and make you a cup of tea before I leave.

Tina nodded her agreement and Crane watched her make her way to the front room, her white tee shirt and comfy jogging bottoms looking creased and unkempt. Just about the same as Tina, really, he thought. But he didn't know what to do about it. Looking down at his watch he wondered how fast he could do the washing up, so he could join Anderson at the crime scene.

The next morning Crane has to pass on the awful details of yet another rape and murder to his Officer Commanding, Captain Edwards.

"I don't bloody believe this, Crane." This time the Captain wasn't red with anger, but white with shock. "Another rape and murder and they think it's a soldier again?"

"Yes, sir, there's no reason not to, really. I reckon it's the same bloke. All the witnesses say he looks like a soldier and Kim said her attacker told her he was as a soldier. The only possible lead we've got is a lad from A Company who was seen entering The Goose alone on Saturday night by the doormen. He fits the general description and Kim said he looked familiar. He's," Crane consulted the file balanced on his lap, "Lance Corporal Yasin Whadi. So I'm going to pull him in later and have a chat with him."

"Alright, but be careful. At the moment you've no evidence against him," Edwards leaned over the table, giving Crane a hard stare.

"I've also got to attend the post mortem later this morning."

"Very well," Edwards relaxed back. "Who's conducting that?"

"Major Martin, thank goodness. So I should get any forensic results quickly and directly, without having to wait for DI Anderson to pass them to me."

Crane and Edwards were both pleased, as Major Martin was a retired army officer who had been an accredited Home Office Pathologist whilst in the fotces. It was therefore a natural progression for him to join the staff at Frimley Park Hospital, on his retirement.

"Right, Crane, before you go, how are you doing with that soldier who said someone was raping and bullying him? Has he come through with any more information?"

"Not yet, sir, Billy wants to set up another meeting with him sometime this week, see how he's feeling and if he feels strong enough to proceed."

"Good. Anything else, Crane?"

"One last thing, sir, could you authorise the sole use of Sally as our team's Office Manager? Billy is trying to keep up with all the paperwork, but it means he isn't investigating and as we've got the biggest cases…"

"Oh, alright, Crane, I'll organise it. On the strict understanding you get results."

"Of course, sir, don't I always?"

Crane left Billy handing over to Sally, whilst he attended the post mortem. As he drove to the hospital, Crane's mood darkened. This was the very thing he didn't want to do, attend the post mortem of another victim. How many more victims could there be before they caught the attacker? His grip tightened on the steering wheel. There were three girls now, Becca Henderson, Kim and the latest victim, Summer Young. As Crane became stuck in a traffic queue on the road from Farnborough to Frimley, he wondered why two girls were killed and yet Kim wasn't? Not that he wished she was, he just wondered why. What was the connection there? Was it because Kim was in the army and the others weren't?

Thinking about Kim made Crane realise that she had a long, slow road to recovery. He couldn't begin to imagine how she must be feeling, but guessed it was pretty much the same as how Turner was feeling. Could both of them manage to turn their lives around? Crane vowed to make both of them understand they could get past this. That part of the healing process must be to see their attacker brought to justice. He knew that rape victims in the past had had a pretty raw deal, with people misunderstanding both the victim and the offense. Crane had to admit to himself that had been his attitude to start with. Thinking the girls somehow deserved what they got for flaunting themselves, dressed in barely-there clothes, high heels and, of course, being drunk. As he inched through the traffic, he realised Kim being raped had made him change his outlook. Not in a million years would she behave as most of the girls did in Aldershot on a Saturday night and yet she had become a victim as well.

By the time the traffic lights changed to green and Crane was able to speed towards the hospital, he was more determined than ever to widen his understanding of rape and most importantly, as far as he was concerned, to get justice for all three girls, by finding the bastard who was doing this.

Chapter 18

Crane eventually battled through the traffic and arrived at Frimley Park Hospital, where he parked his car and rushed to the morgue. Major Martin and DI Anderson were waiting there for him.

"What time do you call this?" Anderson looked at the clock on the wall.

"Not my fault, traffic was bad," Crane grumbled.

"Right then, if we're all ready?" Major Martin cut in, a diminutive man with a razor-sharp mind and saw to match.

"Yes, Major," replied Crane, acknowledging the man's rank, even though he was retired.

The Major spoke into his recorder, whilst Crane and Anderson looked on.

"This is the autopsy of Summer Young. White female, aged 18, body in good condition, well nourished….."

As the Major's voice droned on noting his preliminary observations, Crane looked at the body, making his own. Summer's pale face was untouched. It was the necklace of finger prints she was wearing that was shocking, a ring of large mottled blue and black bruises. Looking down at her naked body, Crane thought Summer looked like she was asleep. But Crane knew that this was her last sleep. She would wake no more.

He thought back to the crime scene yesterday. Summer had lived with her parents in the rural area of Badshot Lea, just outside Aldershot, in a beautiful detached house in its own grounds. Her parents had been away for the week-end and this, together with the isolation of the house, gave her killer plenty of privacy. By the time Crane had arrived, scenes of crime officers were crawling all over the house. Crane stood out of their way, by the open door of Summer's bedroom and looked in. Her body was still in situ and looked sickeningly like that of Becca's, as both girls had long blond hair fanned out over the bed and their clothes torn from their bodies.

Just after Crane arrived at the house, so did her parents and Crane was extremely grateful that, for once, it wasn't his case and he didn't have to break the news to them of their daughter's death. It was harrowing to listen to Derek Anderson asking about their daughter's friends and boyfriends. Did she have a regular boyfriend? No. Did they know of anyone she had fallen out with? No. Did anyone hold a grudge against her? No. The distressing interview had dragged on, without any useful information being gleaned from Summer's parents.

By the time the post mortem finished, Crane felt stifled by the noise and smells particular to the Morgue. Crane and Anderson felt they were no further forward. There was still no forensic evidence. No stray hairs, finger prints or semen, just lubricant from a condom. As Summer had almost certainly been drugged, there was no struggle. No tell-tale skin under her fingertips or blood from scratching her attacker.

"I don't get this, Derek," Crane said as they walked to his car which was parked in the overpriced hospital car park. "Why isn't anyone seeing anything? We were there ourselves on Saturday night and obviously missed him."

"It's because drunken girls are the norm, Crane. It's the perfect cover. No one thinks twice about a boy helping his inebriated girlfriend home."

Crane lit a cigarette.

"No, I suppose not," he said after returning his lighter to his pocket. "I reckon he must have his own car."

"Yes, that's obviously why we're not getting anywhere with the local taxi drivers," Anderson agreed.

"Is there nothing on CCTV that can help us?"

"Sorry, Crane, nothing yet. I've got a couple of detective constables looking through them today and I'll give you a shout if they find anything useful, or even vaguely suspicious."

"I wonder why they do it?" Crane thought aloud.

"Who?" Anderson stopped walking as they arrived at Crane's car.

"The girls. What it is that makes them go completely nuts at the weekend? What's missing in their lives that they have to get so plastered they don't know what they're doing or with whom?"

"Buggered if I know, Crane. Most of the girls we speak to have jobs and are pretty reliable and hard working during the week. I've even known them to be married with kids! It's almost as though they egg each other on. If they don't indulge in stupid drinking contests, drink too much and then boast about it, they're not part of the gang. I wonder if they do it because of peer pressure. Oh well, whatever it is, we can't do anything about it. I'll talk to you later," he finished and grabbed his keys from his pocket.

Anderson was ambling back to his own vehicle when Crane's mobile rang. He listened for a moment, then closing the phone called Anderson back.

"Derek! Here!" Crane waved his mobile in the air. "That was Kim's mother, she needs us to go round to the house right away."

They were watching some banal morning television show, when they heard the plop of the post landing on the floor of the hall, Kim's mother explained, as Kim was too upset to see them.

"I went to check the post, as I was waiting for a letter from my friend Lizzie. You know the one who moved up north a while back. Oh sorry, you wouldn't know that, would you?" Mrs Weston went as pink as her knitted twin set. "Anyway, Kim was chastising me for using what she calls 'snail mail' and said I should use the internet more. I replied I was quite happy with the postal service, thank you very much, as I really like getting letters delivered to the house."

"What actually was delivered, Mrs Weston?" Crane tried very hard not to tap his foot in frustration. But it seemed Mrs Weston was not to be hurried.

"Well, as I picked up the post, Kim offered to make us another cup of coffee as the ones we were drinking had gone cold. So I followed her into the kitchen, with the post in my hand."

Mrs Weston started to walk to the back of the house, as though she was doing a reconstruction of the event, so Crane and Anderson followed her into the kitchen, which was surprisingly modern with a marble topped central island on which was lying a pile of letters.

"Kim was over by the sink, boiling the kettle and putting coffee in our cups," Mrs Weston pointed out the sink. "I sat down here and looked at the post."

She sat on a high stool, so again Crane and Anderson followed her lead and sat.

"Looking at the post," she nodded to the pile of papers and envelopes, "I realised one was for Kim. I remember saying 'here's a letter for you, Kim. It seems at least one of your friends hasn't given up on snail mail'. Of course, Kim wondered who would be sending her a letter. It seemed strange, but I suggested it could be an old school friend."

Crane was itching to look at the small pile of post, but it seemed bad manners to interrupt and anyway Mrs Weston barely paused for breath.

"Well, Kim took the proffered envelope and sat down next to me. She seemed hesitant about opening it, but in the end turned it over and ripped open the envelope, pulling out a small white piece of paper. It's that one on top of the pile here."

"May, I?" asked Anderson and pulled on a set of latex gloves as Mrs Weston nodded.

"Go on," Crane urged Kim's mother who was staring fixated at the note. "What happened next?"

"Kim started to shake. I noticed she had gone very pale and she dropped the letter. She, um, shouted for me to call you, but before I could, Kim seemed to have some sort of seizure. I remember that she stood up and then just sort of collapsed on the floor. It was horrible, like she was having an epileptic fit or something. She, she," Mrs Weston paused to take a deep breath, "she was shaking and mumbling and I didn't know what to do first. You know, ring you as she said or ring the doctor. But, she seemed so ill, so I called the doctor first. I hope that was all right?"

"Of course, Mrs Weston, you absolutely did the right thing," soothed Crane, but as he continued with the platitudes and Mrs Weston prattled on about how Kim had been given a sedative and was resting upstairs in bed, he was far more interested in what Anderson had in his hand. So he stood up and looked over Anderson's shoulder and read:

Where were you Saturday night?
I thought we had a date.
I waited at The Goose but you didn't come.
Be there next week.

Chapter 19

Crane stood smoking in the car park outside his barracks, trying to prioritise his 'to do' list. Going over the events of the last few days was doing his head in. Who would have thought Aldershot could be such a busy place for crime? He remembered Tina once saying that nothing much happened in Aldershot and he'd joked about it being the unknown crime Mecca of the South East of England. But it wasn't a joke anymore. This was all too real. Two rapists - make that one murderer and one rapist - at least he thought there were two rapists. The descriptions in the female rape case were bloody confusing and he still hadn't worked out why that was.

Added to that, one rapist was stalking Kim, who has been reduced to a gibbering wreck. He really must do something about that. She was refusing to see a counsellor, as she seemed to think that would show some sort of implied weakness in her character, or emotional instability. She didn't want anyone other than the team and her immediate family knowing about her assault. Crane guessed she was terrified of it reflecting badly on her army record, hindering any further promotion, or God forbid, resulting in a demotion, if she was not up to the job anymore. At least he'd managed to get indefinite leave for her until the case was solved. Whilst the perpetrator was still on the loose, she was clearly in danger.

The only one in the frame at the moment in Kim's case was a Lance Corporal called Yasin Whadi, originally of Iraqi descent. His family had fled to England many years ago to escape the tyranny of Sadam Hussein. He had to be pulled in and interviewed as soon as possible. Crane had intended to do that yesterday, but what with the post mortem on Summer and then the note left for Kim, there were simply not enough hours in the day.

In the other rape case, Private Turner had finally named his attacker as Lance Corporal Fitch, although he was still refusing to press charges. Anyway they'd no forensic evidence in that case either. Still, Crane thought, there was no harm in keeping a close eye on Fitch. He must arrange that with Staff Sgt Jones.

Crane lit another cigarette promising himself this was the last one before he returned to his office to sort this lot out. He yawned loudly, a reminder that Daniel had colic at the moment, which always seemed to start just as Crane and Tina decided it was time for bed. The resulting screams and sobs keeping them all awake for most of the night. It seemed to Crane that too soon after falling asleep, the alarm clock shrilled and it was time to get up and go to work. It was so upsetting to see Daniel suffering with colic like that. His little body arched, his fists were clenched and he got redder and redder in the face. He was inconsolable in his pain. Crane could now understand why, a few months back, a soldier on guard duty, called Cable, took the opportunity to run home and check on his sick child. However, it resulted in an immediate demotion when he was caught. The battle between duty and family was always a difficult one for soldiers. Stubbing out his cigarette, he took one last lungful of fresh air before returning to his office.

Crane looked up at his team sitting around the conference table in the open plan SIB office. Staff Sgt Jones, his bald head glistening in the overhead lights, Captain Edwards trying to look important by shuffling through his papers, Sgt Billy Williams lounging in his chair, his eyes appraising Sally, who was taking notes and an empty chair where Kim should be. Pulling his eyes away from the empty chair he said, "So we're all agreed then. Jones will organise extra patrols on the streets of Aldershot on Friday and Saturday night - the more men on the ground the better."

"Has DI Anderson approved that, Crane?" Captain Edwards interrupted.

"Of course, sir, he's glad of the extra help," Crane lied smoothly, making a mental note to give Derek the heads up on that one. "So, to continue if I may, sir, or was there anything else you wanted to add?" The sarcasm was clearly not lost on Edwards who glared at Crane but didn't reply.

"Right then, Jones, you're also to keep an eye on Lance Corporal Fitch and Corporal Whadi. Pass their photos out to the lads on guard duty, making sure they report any suspicious behaviour."

"Any more extra duties you want to heap on us, Crane, or is that the lot for now?" Jones growled.

For once Edwards came to Crane's rescue. "Really, Staff Sgt, that's not the attitude." Edwards managed to look and sound haughty at the same time. "We all have to pull together you know. Work as a team…"

"Thank you, sir," Crane interrupted before Edwards could go off on a team building pep talk. "Talking about working as a team…"

"Yes, Sgt Major?" the Captain sounded wary and his eyes narrowed.

"The press, sir. We really need a nominated spokesman from the team. DI Anderson isn't going to be able to keep the lid on the murders much longer."

"I…"

"Thank you, sir, it's very good of you to volunteer. You clearly understand that the rest of us need to be on the ground investigating, in order to produce the high results you have come to expect from us."

"Well,"

"And as you are well aware, my dealings with Diane Chambers of the Aldershot Mail haven't always gone too well in the past. So, I'm sure you want to keep me as far away from her as possible."

"Um,"

"Now, Sgt Williams," Crane cut in over Edwards again.

"Yes, boss?" Billy answered quickly, sitting up and dragging his gaze away from the nubile Sally.

"You're going undercover as a bouncer outside The Goose on Saturday night."

"Does DI…"

Before Edwards could finish his sentence, Crane answered his question, "Yes, sir. DI Anderson is fully apprised of the situation." Which wasn't really an answer but it sounded good. "So, if there's nothing else?" No one spoke. "In that case," Crane finished, "Billy you're with me. We're off to interview Whadi.

Staff Sgt Jones has had him sweating in an interview room on his own for a couple of hours now, so he should be glad of someone to talk to." Crane added as an afterthought, "Oh, if that's all right with you, of course, sir," leaving Edwards opening and closing his mouth like a fish stuck on dry land.

As Crane and Billy entered the room, Crane realised sweating was the right word to describe what Whadi had been doing. The room was unbearably hot, the heating turned up high and the window closed tight. The young soldier stood to attention at their arrival. His light olive skin and dark hair a testament to his Afghani heritage. He was a good looking boy with dark eyes and a strong jaw line. Crane could see how the ladies could fall for his smooth skin and no doubt equally smooth pick-up lines.

"Ah, Lance Corporal Whadi isn't it?"

"Sir."

"Sit down then, lad, make yourself comfortable." A sarcastic statement that Billy smiled at, as there was only one hard plastic, very uncomfortable chair available, that Whadi had just jumped up from.

The Lance Corporal sat rigidly as though still to attention and Crane and Billy joined him at the table.

"We," Crane indicated Billy, "are investigating a particularly nasty crime with the Aldershot Police. It's one that you may be able to help us with."

"How, sir?" Yasin spoke into the silence that Crane had let develop.

"Well, we understand you are a regular at The Goose pub in Aldershot."

Whadi didn't reply and looked nervously from one man to the other.

"That is correct isn't it, Lance Corporal?" Billy said.

"Um, yes, sir, I suppose."

"You were there last Saturday night?" Crane asked.

"I think so, sir."

"Think so? Can't you do better than that?"

"Ah, let me see..."

Billy took his turn, "I'd say it was pretty definite that you were there, seeing as how we have a witness."

Crane watched the Lance Corporal blanch, his olive skin turning a few shades lighter.

"What do you say now, Lance Corporal?"

"Yes, sir, I was at The Goose on Saturday night."

"Who did you meet there?" Billy's hand was poised over his notebook.

"Just a few of the lads, sir."

"Give us their names then."

As Whadi gave the names of three friends who were purportedly with him on Saturday night and Billy wrote them down, Crane watched Whadi closely. "Anyone else?" he asked.

"Sir?"

"Did you meet anyone else there?"

"No, sir." Whadi's eyes slid away from Crane's gaze.

"No girls? A good looking bloke like you must pull the birds."

"No, sir, no girls," Whadi said to the floor.

Crane thought for a moment and then said, "Okay, we'll just check these names out, then you can go back to your unit."

Crane and Billy left Whadi alone with his thoughts in the sweat box. As they stood in the corridor, Billy said, "What do you think, boss?"

"Something's off there."

"That's what I thought. His eyes are all over the

place."

"Yes, especially when I mentioned girls. Check out those lads, Billy. If they all agree they met him in The Goose, pull them in to take statements. See what they have to say about Whadi. Work with Staff Sgt Jones. Let me know what happens."

"Sir."

Billy returned to the SIB office, as Crane went outside to think, while he smoked a cigarette.

A letter to Billy

Hi Billy,

Thanks for meeting me earlier. Sorry I made you walk so far around Ash Ranges. It's just that I wanted to pick a spot where we wouldn't be overheard. And we weren't. We didn't meet another soul the whole time we were there. I find it very peaceful amongst the trees on the Ranges. If you sit still long enough, you can watch squirrels foraging for nuts and spot rabbits popping in and out of their holes. Nature has a calming effect on me, not surprising, I suppose, as people don't.

I finally told you the name of my attacker whilst we were there. Lance Corporal Fitch. It's strange knowing that someone else shares your secret, that I have nothing to hide from you. It makes me feel vulnerable.

I don't always know what to say to you and Sgt Major Crane. I know you have questions, concerns, things you want to ask to me, but I'm not ready for conversations like that. I don't yet know how to talk about my feelings. I still find it easier to put words down on paper, instead of into my mouth.

I realise you are both trying very hard to understand what has happened to me. But I can see in your faces that you are having trouble relating to me. Or is it perhaps that you are finding these conversations as difficult as I am, but from an entirely different *perspective. Your focus has to be on catching the man responsible for this disgusting crime.*

I liken my situation to a battle. Only I'm not fighting the enemy, but one of my own. One of the people I'd always been told had my back. That betrayal, the betrayal from someone not only in my unit, but in command, is almost worse than the sexual assault itself.

Chapter 20

The quietness of the church enveloped Crane as he went from the bright sunshine outside, into the gloom of the interior. Although not a religious man, Crane had great respect for the army Padres, who work tirelessly with the troops both at home and abroad. And great respect for one in particular, Padre Simmons, who Crane was hoping to find in his office.

As Crane threaded his way through the massive structure that was the Army Garrison Church, he couldn't help remembering his previous encounters in the building, both with Padre Symmonds and an unwelcome attacker. A case that put the lives of Crane and the Padre in danger, as they pursued an egotistical maniac who was encouraging soldiers to follow the steps to Heaven.

By now Crane had reached the Padre's office, whose voice he had been following through the stone corridors. At first Crane thought the Padre was in a meeting with someone, but soon realised he must be practicing his next sermon. So he stood outside the door, waiting until there was a break in the oratory, before knocking.

"Come in," Padre Symmonds called. "Ah, Crane, good to see you."

The Padre came from around his desk to shake Crane's hand. Padre Symmonds was dressed in a black clerical shirt with his white dog collar and army uniform trousers. His hair was the regulation short length, although he sported rather an old fashioned cut for a youngish Captain. It made him look a bit geeky, which Crane supposed the Padre was, come to think of it. Yes, fastidious and over cautious. Someone who would only work strictly within army rules and regulations.

"Good to see you as well, sir," Crane said. "Sorry, was I interrupting a practice session?"

Going slightly pink the Padre said, "Well, yes, I do like to rehearse before a particularly important sermon."

"So do I, sir, rehearse that is, normally before a particularly important conversation with my wife, otherwise I tend to fluff my lines," Crane grinned.

"So, what brings you here? Do you want to arrange a christening? I hear congratulations are in order." The Padre returned to his seat behind his desk, grabbing his diary.

"Oh, for Daniel you mean? No, sir, not yet. Tina and I are concentrating on getting this parenting thing right at the moment. We've not had time to think about christenings, although you do have a point, sir. It's something we must get around to doing."

"Excellent news, I'd love to have you all here and be a small part of young Daniel's life. Just come along and book a date when you're ready," he indicated the diary, which he put back in the desk drawer.

"Thank you, sir. I'll talk to Tina. But the real reason for my visit is a rather more delicate matter than a christening I'm afraid."

"Well, you best sit down then."

Crane looked around the Padre's office, which was much neater than last time he was here. The wardrobe doors were open and Crane saw the clerical vestments neatly lined up on hangers, together with the Padre's army uniform. The bookcase, whilst still crammed, appeared to be set out in category order. Behind the Padre's green baize covered desk, hung a cross and on the opposite wall, a picture of the Queen. Crane grabbed a chair, sat at the old fashioned desk and leaned in to tell the Padre all about his current case and the attack on Kim.

"My goodness me, how appalling, poor Kim," the young Padre said, after hearing the bones of the case. His face screwed up in consternation, "But I don't see how I can help your investigation."

"No, sir, I don't need help with the investigation this time. I was wondering if you could go and see Kim. She's in a pretty bad way, especially after receiving these notes, which are purportedly from her attacker. She won't see a counsellor and is terrified that there could be a mention of mental illness on her army record. But she has to talk to someone. I need her to see that she can climb out of this awful black hole she's in. Try and get her to use her army training, her pride in her military achievements, to understand how strong she is. So maybe if you let her know that you are willing to have a few off the record chats, it may work. She's having flashbacks and her symptoms are very similar to post traumatic stress disorder. I'm sure you've talked to some of the lads who suffered from it on their return from Afghanistan."

"I see. You're right about my experience in this field, unfortunately, but you don't think the fact I'm a man will frighten her? Maybe she would respond better to a woman."

"Actually, no, sir, I don't. I think she will be able to look beyond the man bit and see the man of God, if you get my meaning."

"Very well, Crane, I'll see what I can do."

"Thank you, sir."

Crane pushed a piece of paper across to the Padre, with Kim's contact details on it. "Oh," Crane remembered as he got up to leave, "for goodness sake don't tell her I sent you will you? In fact don't tell anyone I sent you."

"Alright, Crane, whatever you say."

As Crane left the office, he glanced back and saw the Padre pulling counselling books off his shelf.

Chapter 21

After his unofficial visit to the Padre, Crane returned to his car and drove to Aldershot Police Station, the monolithic structure of grey concrete that successive Town Councils had planned to knock down and completely rebuild. But those plans had never come to fruition, because of the economic recession, or lack of interest from retail sponsors. Aldershot was still suffering the backlash of the Parachute Regiment being relocated from Aldershot over ten years ago. A move the town had never really recovered from. No longer being the 'home of the British Army' had weakened the local economy drastically. And now with further cutbacks to the military being planned, who knew what would happen to Aldershot.

Of course Aldershot Garrison hosting a Team GB training camp for the London 2012 Olympic athletes and Paralympians, had helped raise the profile of Aldershot. But that was a transient time, the population of Aldershot swelling for a month or so whilst the athletes were there and then shrinking back once again to normal low levels. A boost in employment at the camp helped, but the accompanying thefts didn't say much for the good name of the local population. Crane grinned as he remembered a particular nasty pair of women he caught stealing jewellery from athletes staying in St Omer Barracks, or St Omer Village as the army like to call it now. He read in the local paper last week, with some satisfaction, that they'd been given prison sentences for their crimes.

After parking his car, Crane walked into the station and was waved through to DI Anderson's office in CID.

"Ah, Crane, just in time for tea."

Anderson was drinking from a cup and had a couple of sugary cakes on a plate.

"Want one?" he asked, pushing the plate towards Crane.

"No thanks, Derek, constant battle with my waistline."

Crane patted his flat stomach and sat down in front of the desk.

"Don't worry about that much myself," Derek replied, patting his own stomach, which his shirt was straining to cover.

"But you're not in the army, are you, Derek?"

"No, thank God."

Anderson finished his cake and wiped the crumbs off his fingers with a handkerchief that he stuffed back into his trouser pocket. Placing his arms on his desk and leaning on them, he asked, "Right, where are we on the rape cases?"

Crane firstly relayed details of his interview with Yasin Whadi. "So, I reckon I could have a prime suspect with the Afghan," he finished.

"The Afghan?"

"Sorry, didn't I tell you? His parents are Afghani."

"No you didn't and anyway it shouldn't make any difference what his ethnic background is," Anderson drained his cup of tea, smacking his lips appreciatively.

"Well, I suppose you could look at it like that. Anyway that's not important. What is important is that he looks a good bet to me. Very cagey, not giving anything away. Looks and acts guilty."

"And you've deduced all this from an initial interview have you, Crane?"

"Well, in case you've forgotten I do have some experience with Afghanis," Crane leaned back in his chair and crossed his legs. "I've served over there, trying to train their police force and of course there was that debacle while the Team GB athletes were here. Shifty lot, I've always found."

"Well, in case you've forgotten, I particularly asked to be in on any interviews you conduct in relation to this case. A police case, remember?"

"Oh dear, did you? Sorry, my mistake," Crane tried to hide the smirk threatening to break on his face. "Anyway," he continued, trying to distract Anderson from the interview with Whadi, "let's talk about Kim. The thing that bothers me is how did this bloke know Kim was staying with her mum? If he only picked her at random on the night of the attack, he'd have no idea that her mother lived in the area."

"You've got a point there, Crane. Maybe he's been stalking her for a while before he plucked up the courage to talk to her. Her being in The Goose that particular Saturday seems to have been good luck for him and bad luck for Kim, as she's not a regular there. Is Kim close to her parents?"

"It seems so. She visits them a couple of times a week, so if he was keeping an eye on her, he would have easily found out that her mum and dad live in the area."

Anderson shivered, "Gives you the creeps doesn't it? You know, the thought of someone keeping tabs on you without your knowledge."

"Maybe some nosey neighbour in the street has noticed a young man hanging around? Someone who's not from the area," Crane fingered his scar. "Is there any chance of another quick knock around the neighbouring properties?"

"Alright, I'll ask about descriptions, a dark-haired young man and a fair-haired one."

"Best keep this quiet from Kim, Derek. No point in freaking her out yet again."

They then turned to the plan of action for Saturday night. Anderson was happy about the increased RMP on the roads of Aldershot, as Crane expected he would be. Let's face it, Crane reasoned, at the moment Anderson needed all the help he could get.

They were just agreeing that Billy was to do a stint on the door at The Goose, when a young DC put his head round the door. "Sorry to bother you, Guv, Diane Chambers from the Aldershot Mail is making a right nuisance of herself downstairs," he said. "She insists on speaking to the DI in charge of the rape cases."

"Oh, very well, put her in an interview room and I'll be down in a few minutes." Turning to Crane he asked, "Do you want to come too?"

"Not bloody likely," Crane replied. "I'll just sit here for a few minutes until she's safely out of the way, then I'll leave."

"Coward," laughed Anderson as he left his office.

While Crane was waiting, he pulled out his mobile and called Billy.

"Have you an update for me on the interviews with those friends of Yasin?"

"Yes, boss, I was just going to call you. One of the lads said he saw Yasin talking to a young white girl in The Goose. Getting very pally they were too."

Chapter 22

The night was drawing in as Crane pulled up outside his quarter, reminding him it would soon be November. The wind whipped at his coat as he climbed out of the car and then reached back in for his briefcase. If he got a chance, he wanted to go over the statements Billy had taken from Yasin Whadi's friends about their night out at The Goose last Saturday. Of course, that all depended on what he found behind the front door tonight. Sometimes Tina was organised, happy and relaxed and at other times she was dishevelled, the chores undone and Daniel very fretful. If it was a bad night he wouldn't be able to get any work done, he'd have to concentrate on helping Tina.

Crane opened the front door, entering cautiously, not wanting to bang in and shout hello for fear of waking the baby when Tina had only just got him settled. He no sooner put his briefcase on the floor when he heard a wail coming from the kitchen. Shit, a bad night, then, he decided.

Walking into the kitchen, he saw Daniel sat in his bouncer, red faced, fists clenched and back arched. The kitchen looked like a bomb had hit it, as did Tina. Her hair, once scraped back, was now falling in tendrils around her face, her blouse was covered in milk splashes and she was as red in the face as Daniel.

"Oh, Tom, thank goodness," tears welled in her eyes. "I can't get him to take the colic drops."

"Alright, love, I'll get him."

Crane gave Tina a quick kiss before scooping the child from his carrier.

"Here, quick!"

Tina passed him a piece of muslin but it was too late. Daniel had thrown up all down the back of his suit jacket. Turning, Crane was relieved to see his wife laugh at the sight of him with a screaming baby over his shoulder and vomited milk all down his jacket and joined in the laughter.

"I'll take him upstairs and clean the both of us up. Why don't you sort yourself and the kitchen out and then phone for a take-away."

"Only if I can choose," she replied.

"Choose away," he called as he went up the stairs.

The baby was calmer after burping up some of the trapped wind in his stomach and Crane managed to get him to take the colic drops and then cleaned them both up. He spent some time walking around the house with Daniel on his shoulder; rubbing his back and holding him close to help alleviate the pain of the colic. As he wandered, Tina sorted herself out and phoned for a Chinese take-away.

With the baby asleep at last, they dished up their meal.

"Sorry," Tina said as she wrapped some Peking duck into a pancake, "for not having everything ready when you got home. I'm not very good at this mothering bit am I?"

"Oh, Tina, of course you are," Crane took hold of her hand. "Any baby can get colic and it's bloody awful for the baby and for the mother. Stop feeling guilty the whole time. You're doing a great job."

Crane was not sure where he got these nuggets of information from, but hey, he thought, they sounded good and would hopefully give Tina some much needed confidence.

"Yes, but I should be able to cope without you having to chip in. I'm the one at home for Christ's sake. All I have to do is look after the house and the baby and I can't even do that properly."

She took a gulp of the red wine Crane had just poured for her.

"Tina, stop it. You don't have to be superwoman, super mum or super anything else. Daniel's my son as well. I want to take part in his care as much as I can. I don't want to be pushed to the sidelines with you being focused on the baby and nothing else."

"But -"

"No, Tina, no buts. I know I can't be here all the time, but when I am I need to be part of this family, not some outsider looking in."

"Thank you, Tom."

"There's nothing to thank me for. Anyway, talking about times when I'm not here, sorry, but I'm going to be out next Saturday night again," and Crane went on to update Tina on his cases.

"Poor Kim," Tina said as she cleared away the food cartons. "Do you think I should visit? I could take the baby. Maybe that would cheer her up, or if nothing else, give her a good laugh at my ineptitude. And it would get me out of the house. What do you think?"

"I think that's a lovely idea. I'll go and ring her mum,

see what she says. Oh, by the way," he remembered, "Padre Symmonds asked about Daniel being christened today. Why don't you think about it? Perhaps see your mum and together come up with some plans."

Grateful that Tina now had other things to think about and look forward to, Crane went to make his phone call.

Chapter 23

Crane threw a file onto Anderson's desk in disgust, the following Monday morning.

"I don't bloody believe it, another victim. This is getting ridiculous, Derek."

They had just returned to Aldershot Police Station from the crime scene, a shared flat in North Camp. A student, Jackie Glass, had found the body of her fellow student Madison Denton when she returned to their flat in the early hours of Monday morning, after visiting her parents in High Wycombe for the weekend. According to her statement, Jackie had crept in around 02:00 hours as she didn't want to wake up her flat mate. However, when she passed Madison's room the door was open. Peering in, she saw her sprawled on top of her bed. Thinking it strange that Madison would fall asleep half-naked like that, she went in to make sure her friend was alright. But, of course, she wasn't.

"Seems to me things are spiralling out of control."

Crane watched Anderson run his hand through his hair in a vain attempt to control it. But Anderson could no more control his hair, than they could control the current spate of murders.

"I don't see how the rapist gets past us all. Billy was on the door at The Goose, there were extra RMP and police patrolling the streets and not one person seems to have seen him supporting a drunken girl."

"That's the problem, though, isn't it? How many times in one night do you see a drunken girl being helped home? Talk about blending in. I tell you he'd stand out more if he acted sober. There aren't many sober young people out there at eleven o'clock on a Saturday night."

"Are you doing the usual checks?"

"Don't start, Crane. Of course we are. What do you take me for? I've got uniformed officers going round Madison's neighbours. Detective constables are talking to the local taxi firms and office staff are checking CCTV, both from Victoria Street and in the vicinity of the flat in North Camp. What the hell else am I supposed to do?"

"Alright, sorry," Crane said as he looked at his watch. "Look, its 10:00hours, lets get down to Frimley Park Hospital where Major Martin is doing the post mortem. Maybe he'll have something for us. I bloody well hope he has, before I have to face Captain Edwards."

Major Martin had already started the post mortem, by the time Crane and Anderson arrived.

"Hello, you two, I was wondering if anyone was going to bother coming this morning."

"Sorry, sir," Crane said, "we're a bit busy at the moment."

"Bloody right you are, Crane. What's this, the third victim?"

"The third one killed, fourth victim counting Kim."

"Dear God. Right well, let's see if we can find anything that might help you," and the Major returned to his task.

As Crane watched the Major cut, saw and poke, he saw there were more bruises on Madison than on the other girls. Her blond hair was a tangled mess, some of her finger nails were broken and there were bruises on her arms and the inside of her thighs.

"It looks like she put up a bit of a fight, Derek. See all those bruises?"

"Yes and as you saw, her room's in a state as well. Lamps knocked over, bed a right mess, that sort of thing."

"I think she came round a bit at some point during the rape," observed Major Martin. "There's definite defensive bruising. I'm hopeful I'll get some skin from under her fingernails to test for DNA. If there is any, your boy could have scratches on him."

"How come the drug didn't work as well with Madison, Major? Sorry, sir, I'm assuming she was drugged as well."

"Looks like she was, Crane, but you know you'll have to wait for the test results to be definite. Anyway, the trouble is, drugging someone is not an exact science. It depends on several factors. The amount of the drug she was given, the amount of alcohol she consumed before hand, her normal consumption of alcohol and, of course, her height and weight. Usually the girl is left pliable and unable to remember anything until well into the following day. However, in this case, it looks like he didn't give her enough to start with."

"What do you mean, to start with?"

"Well, she's not been strangled as there's no bruising around her neck and her hyoid bone is intact. At the moment my best guess is that he gave her some more of the drug when she started to come round. But with what she'd consumed earlier, it became a fatal dose. I think she died of an overdose, but again I'll be in a better position to confirm that when I've got the toxicology results back."

By now the Major had worked his way down Madison's body to her pubic hair. As he ran a comb through it he shouted, "Got you!"

"Sir?"

The Major was holding something aloft in a pair of tweezers.

"There's a black hair nestling in her blond pubic hair. It looks like it has a root on it. We should get DNA from this."

"Finally, we've got a piece of forensic evidence," Anderson smiled through his tiredness, his face looking as saggy as a bulldog's.

"Yes, but how long before we get the results? If it's going to be several weeks, he could strike again during that time."

"Thank you for your optimism, Crane," the Major commented. "Don't worry, I'll put it through as a rush job, bugger the budget."

Crane slowly climbed the stairs to Captain Edwards' office. He knew before he got there he was going to get a bollocking. Entering the office, he stood to attention in front of Edwards' desk, who made him wait for some moments before he lifted his haughty head to stare at Crane.

"Ah, Crane. Bit of a disaster area this isn't it? I've just been reading this report of yours."

Edwards threw the offending piece of paper across

his desk towards Crane.

"Sir."

"Another rape and murder."

"Sir."

"By the same attacker, the one who everyone thought was a soldier."

"Sir." Crane was still standing to attention, not having been given permission to stand at ease, nor sit.

"Do you know what I've been doing all morning, Crane?"

"No, sir," Crane answered the rhetorical question, winding Edwards up even more.

"Fire fighting, Sgt Major, that's what I've been doing. Fielding press calls and calls from the brass. The only thing I could do with both parties was to agree that the lack of progress was totally unacceptable. Do you understand Sgt Major? Totally un-ac-cept-a-ble!" The Captain shouted every syllable.

Crane wondered if Edwards was going to have a heart attack. His face had gone a funny puce colour. He hoped not; he didn't fancy giving him mouth to mouth resuscitation.

"Sir."

"Now get out of my bloody office and get some results."

"Sir." Crane took it that he was dismissed and did as he was told, leaving the Captain's office to return to his own, but via the car park for a cigarette, naturally.

A letter to Sgt Major Crane

Sir,

I firstly want to apologise. Apologise for my behaviour, for being a coward, for being ashamed of what has happened. I know I should be able to sort it out myself, fend for myself, after all that's what real men do isn't it?

Maybe if I'd stood up to Fitch in the first place, none of this would have happened. I should have just punched him, that first time, but I was too afraid. Afraid of the consequences of hitting someone of a higher rank than myself. That alone tells me I am weak, no longer a man, not as strong or assertive as I should have been.

But finally I am able to stand up to him. This is my revenge for what he has done to me. Turning him in. Showing everyone what sort of man he is. Shaming him as he has shamed me.

But all this thinking about it is making me angry. Angry at Fitch. Angry at the army. Even angry at you lot for taking so long to do anything about it. You're 'keeping an eye on him'. What fucking good is that? You need to arrest him, question him do something – anything!

Chapter 24

Crane entered the interview room, closing the door behind him with exaggerated care, before turning to face the young man standing to attention at the table. DI Anderson had already taken his place opposite Yasin Whadi.

Standing by the door and staring at Whadi, Crane saw the young man, dressed in his fatigues, straining to hold his position. Beads of sweat were popping up on his forehead, the sinews in his neck straining and his fists clenched by his side. Another sure sign of guilt, Crane thought.

"At ease, Lance Corporal," Crane barked.

Some of the tension drained away as Whadi relaxed into the at ease position. Legs opens and arms behind his back.

"You may sit, Lance Corporal."

As the Lance Corporal fell into his chair he started fiddling, firstly with his tunic, then his hair and finally his fingers.

Throughout, Anderson had been looking on, a wry smile of amusement on his face. "After all that palaver, are we ready, Crane?"

Scowling at Anderson, Crane sat next to him, taking some moments to shrug off his jacket and place it over the back of the chair, before he spoke.

"Right, Lance Corporal. I take it you know why you're here again?"

"No, sir, not really. Has it something to do with me going to The Goose?"

"Damn right it has," Crane growled.

Then changing tack he leaned back in his chair.

"By the way, your alibi checks out," he said and indicated the file he'd put in front of him on the table.

Yasin nodded, blinking rapidly and his shoulders drooped with relief.

"But one of your friends said something very interesting."

Crane opened the file, pulled out a statement, looking first at the paper and then at Whadi.

"He did, sir?"

Crane saw Whadi's eye widen at that piece of information.

"Yes," Anderson started a double act with Crane. "We understand you were seen chatting to a young blond-haired girl that night."

"Was I, sir?" Yasin didn't seem sure who he was answering, so his head swivelled from Anderson to Crane and back.

"Yes. And a young blond-haired woman was found dead the day after in her bedsit," continued Anderson.

Whadi's mouth remained firmly closed.

"Were you in The Goose this past Saturday, Lance Corporal?" asked Crane.

"Well, um, I'm not sure, sir," a smile played at the corners of the young man's mouth.

"Why not?"

"Um, drink. I had quite a bit to drink, trying to blot out all this business," Whadi nodded his head at the two men interviewing him.

"So you were drinking in Aldershot on Saturday night, then?"

"I guess."

"Interesting that, wouldn't you say, Inspector?" Crane looked at Anderson.

"Very, Sgt Major, considering another young blond girl was raped and murdered on Saturday night."

"And a black hair was found on her body," said Crane. "What do you make of that, Lance Corporal?"

Whadi didn't answer, simply stared at them.

"You have dark hair don't you Whadi?" Crane pushed.

The young man merely nodded.

"I'm sure forensic tests will confirm that it's one of yours."

Crane spoke with authority, sure in his deduction, even though any DNA test results wouldn't be available for some time.

"That's not possible!" Whadi jumped to his feet in rage.

"Lance Corporal, remember who you're talking to," Crane snarled, forcing Whadi to sit down on his chair. "If it's not possible, then why do we have witnesses saying they saw you chatting up the victim?" Crane was once again stretching the facts.

"They must be wrong, sir," Whadi hissed.

"Really?" Crane asked. "Then why are there unsolved rape cases in two towns near to where you were previously posted?"

"I've no idea what you're talking about, sir," Whadi said shaking his head.

"Well, if you're as innocent as you say you are, then you'll let me have a DNA sample, won't you, Lance Corporal?"

Yasin stared at Crane for a moment and then nodded his agreement.

Crane stood and went over to the door. Opening it, he called though to the office for Staff Sgt Jones. As Jones arrived Crane looked down at the young man with disgust and said, "Lance Corporal Yasin Whadi here has agreed to a DNA test, Staff Sgt. Would you do the honours please? After that the Lance Corporal is free to return to his Unit."

As the young man was led away, Anderson watched in silence. Once Whadi and Jones were out of the room he said, "So that's how you do things in the army is it, Crane? You've not got any evidence, really, you know. That was all bluff and bluster."

"That may be so, Derek, but I'm going for a confession. I'll get the forensic evidence to back it up later on."

As Crane turned to leave, Billy put his head round the door.

"Sorry to disturb you, sir. You and the DI are wanted round at Kim's mums. Yet another incident, I'm afraid."

Crane screeched to a halt outside the house, yanking on the hand brake and flinging himself out of the car. Anderson got out of the other side at a more leisurely pace. As Crane hurried through the garden gate, the front door of the house was opened, much to Crane's surprise, by Captain Symmonds.

"Sir, I understand something's happened. Is Kim alright?" Crane tried to peer around the Padre.

"Well, Crane, I suppose she's alright, under the circumstances. At the moment she's upstairs asleep. I made her take one of the tablets the doctor left last time."

"Jesus Christ, oh sorry, sir," Crane mumbled an apology for his blasphemy. "What happened?"

"Come into the front room."

The Padre turned and led the way. Crane noted the Captain was out of uniform and without his dog collar. He must have wanted to project a less threatening figure to Kim, in the hope she would open up to him, Crane deduced.

As Crane and Anderson filed into the room, they could see broken glass lying on the floor, mingling with the carpet fibres, glistening in the sunlight streaming through the big hole in the bay window. A brick lay in the centre of the mess, a splash of terracotta against the beige carpet. On the floor by the Padre's feet was a sheet of white crumpled paper.

"I called round to see Kim, as you suggested, Crane," the Padre explained. "She got up from the chair to go and make us a cup of tea, when the pane of glass just, just exploded." Captain Symmonds shook his head. "Luckily we were both too far away for the glass to cause us any injury. But then Kim saw this piece of paper," Symmonds indicated it with his head. "She picked it up, looked at it in horror and then started screaming. I couldn't get her to stop, so her mother gave her one of those tablets. What a shock, Crane. I don't know, how come whenever I work with you, I end up being put in danger?" The Padre tried a lame attempt at humour; a reference to his undercover work with the local churches a few months ago.

"Who's handled the note, Padre?".

"Oh, only Kim. She dropped it on the floor here and I haven't touched it. I guessed it could be evidence. I don't know what it says."

"Thank you, sir, it was the right thing to do."

Anderson snapped on latex gloves, before bending to pick up the offending piece of paper with one hand. With the other he fumbled to get a plastic cover out of his pocket. As he slipped the note inside it, all three men peered at the large scrawling handwriting.

Where were you on Saturday? I waited but you didn't come.
Why are you doing this?
This is your last chance!
Meet me next week or I'll come and find you.
That's a promise.

Chapter 25

As Crane inserted the key into his front door, the shoulders he had been trying to keep up all day, sagged. He hated what was happening to Kim. He felt so responsible. She was one of his team and he was doing a bloody awful job of keeping her safe. He'd got to come up with something to find the bastard who was doing this. Perhaps his brain would work a bit better after some food and a drink.

Swinging open the door he stepped through, putting down his briefcase, but not bothering to take off his coat, for silence greeted his arrival. The lights were on in the house, but as he stood still and listened, no cooking sounds met his ears, nor smells his nose. He pushed open the door to the lounge, to find Tina asleep on the settee, Daniel spread across her chest, Tina's arms holding him safe. Trying not to trip over toys and other baby paraphernalia, he turned off the overhead lights, leaving a small lamp glowing for when Tina woke up.

The kitchen didn't look any more inviting. Half empty coffee mugs littered the surfaces, mingling with used bottles. The coffee percolator had burnt coffee crusting in the bottom of the jug and Crane turned the machine off before it was completely ruined. Opening the fridge he found bottles of baby milk, but precious little else. Closing the door instead of slamming it, which was what he really wanted to do, he turned and left the house.

"Tom, Tom, wake up!"

Crane bolted upright on the sofa, instantly awake and looked at Tina, who was wrapping her dressing gown around her and tying the belt.

"What, where, what time is it?"

"It's half past six. The alarm clock woke me up. You'd better go and have a shower and get ready for work. I'll make coffee. And be quiet – don't wake Daniel," shouted Tina, loud enough to wake him herself.

"Shit," Crane said as Tina left the room. He grabbed his suit jacket from the floor and followed her at a more sedate pace, as his head was banging. Standing at the kitchen door and leaning against the frame for support, he asked, "Do we have any headache tablets?"

Tina's response was to pull open a kitchen drawer, grab the packet and throw it at him, banging the drawer closed afterwards.

"Shit," said Crane to himself again, as he dropped the box of tablets. Bending down slowly and picking it up, he clutched the packet to his chest and dragged himself upstairs with the aid of the banister.

He was back in the kitchen in twenty minutes, damp and exhausted, but ready for work. He fell into a chair and grabbed the mug of black coffee Tina had put on the table for him.

"Sgt's Mess?" Tina asked.

"Mmm," Crane answered.

"Because?"

"Because you were asleep and I didn't want to disturb you."

"Try again, Tom."

"Because there was nothing to eat and nothing in the fridge to make anything with, so I thought I'd grab something to eat at the Mess."

"Looks to me like all you grabbed was beer."

"Maybe I had one or two too many."

"For God's sake, Tom, couldn't you have helped instead of running away?" Tina turned away from him. "I know I'm a bloody awful wife and mother but you didn't need to rub it in. Making me feel even more of a failure than I do already." Tina scrabbled in her dressing gown pocket for a tissue and blew her nose.

"Tina, for God's sake, not everything is your fault, you know. I had a crappy day and needed to let off a bit of steam, that's all. Don't make any more of it than that."

"What about my crappy day, though, Tom?" Tina turned on him. "I'd clearly had a crappy day as well. But there's nowhere for *me* to go and let off a bit of steam on my own, is there?"

"Alright, so we're both under pressure. Okay? Look I haven't got time for this, Tina, I've got to get to work."

Crane stood up, moving towards her to kiss her goodbye.

As if on cue, Daniel started to cry from the nursery upstairs. Pushing past Crane, Tina went upstairs without speaking to him and without kissing him. So Crane poured his coffee down the sink and left for work.

Chapter 26

Crane took a deep breath before knocking on the door to the house. He was not at all sure how he was going to handle this, so had brought Captain Symmonds along for moral and, hopefully, verbal support.

Kim herself opened the door, immediately putting Crane on the back foot, as he was expecting her mother.

"Hello, sir?" the question in Kim's voice unavoidable.

"Hi, Kim, um, we wondered if we could have a word with you?" he asked, but the words came out in a rush and he looked at Captain Symmonds.

"Is that alright, Kim?" the Captain asked and as she nodded, the two men followed her through to the sitting room.

Crane decided that Kim was beginning to look a little better. Her hair had been freshly washed and she was dressed in a tee shirt and jeans, rather than being covered from neck to foot in her track suit. However, she was still not making eye contact with either man.

Once they were all seated she asked, "Do you have any more information for me, sir? About the latest note, I mean."

"More info yes, but no leads I'm afraid." Crane leaned forwards towards Kim who was sitting in an armchair opposite him. "A neighbour reports hearing a crash and then what she thought was the sound of a motor bike racing away. She didn't see anything, though, so no leads there. I'm afraid we have no idea who threw the brick with the note through the window, nor what sort of bike they were on."

"What about forensics, sir?"

"Still no match to the DNA off the hair follicle we found on, um, we found. I've taken a DNA sample from a suspect we have in custody, for comparison, but I'm still waiting on the results," he finished, trying to disguise the awkwardness he felt. But he probably wasn't fooling anybody he realised.

"So?" Kim asked.

"Pardon?"

"So, why are you really here, sir?"

Crane stood and began pacing around the room.

"We really need some help, Kim. This can't be allowed to go on. The rapes, the murders, this continued stalking."

He saw Kim's face drain of colour but ploughed on.

"I've hatched a plan, but I need your co-operation." He stood still and stared at her. "All I want you to do for now, is to listen to what I've got to say. Will you do that for me, Kim?"

He watched Kim sit up just that little bit straighter as she said, "Yes, sir."

Crane sat back down and went on to outline his plan. He explained he wanted Kim to go to The Goose on Saturday night, to try and flush out this maniac. She wouldn't be alone. Billy would be there, as would DI Anderson and Crane. Staff Sgt Jones would be outside around the corner and quite a few of the RMP lads would be undercover in the bar. Or at least as undercover as an RMP could be, he had to admit, which raised a smile from Kim.

"I can arrange for you to go with a specially trained police officer, a female one and a couple of WPC's so you'd go as a group of girls."

"No, I don't think so, sir."

Crane sank back into his seat.

"It's alright, I do understand, Kim," but Crane failed to keep the disappointment out of his voice.

"No, sir, you've misunderstood. I don't want to go with a few WPCs who I don't know and don't understand me and how I'm feeling. I want to go with a male escort. I'd feel a lot safer."

Crane leaned forward again.

"Of course, Kim, anyone, who…" Crane stopped speaking as he saw Kim was looking at Padre Symmonds.

"Would you accompany me, sir?" she asked the Padre.

As the Captain nodded his assent, Crane couldn't resist saying, "Very well, but without your clerical collar please, sir."

"We're doing what?" Anderson shouted from his desk in the CID office, where Crane was lounging nonchalantly against the door frame.

"A bit of an undercover operation on Saturday night, with Kim."

"Are you lot in the army all mad, Crane? I can't believe this."

Anderson shook his head, his hair flying around as though he was sitting outside in a strong wind.

"Well, we're doing it with or without you, Derek. With would be preferable, of course, but..." Crane shrugged.

"And Kim's agreed? Are you sure you've not bullied her into this?" Anderson cut across Crane's little show of bravado, narrowing his eyes and looking suspicious.

"What do you take me for, Derek? I'm not that manipulative!"

"Really?" Anderson snorted.

"Really. Now are you in or not?"

Anderson reluctantly agreed, as Crane always knew he would and they got on with working out the details of their plan. Crane took off his jacket while Anderson ordered cups of tea. After scribbling notes and drawing impromptu layouts out of The Goose, they plotted where each surveillance group would stand. Anderson had a list of instructions for the policemen and women and Crane for the RMP. They were just winding up their meeting when Crane's mobile rang.

"Crane," he answered. He hadn't looked at the caller display and was therefore surprised when it was Tina. At least he thought it was her, speaking between sobs.

"Tom, where are you? Can you come?" she wailed in his ear.

"Tina, what the hell's the matter? Of course I can come, are you at home?"

"No," she gulped. "T, T, Tesco."

"I'll be there in five minutes."

Crane closed the phone, grabbed his suit jacket and ran out of Anderson's office, without any explanation and without his paperwork.

Chapter 27

Crane pulled up as near to the front door of Tesco as he could get, leaping out of the car and running to Tina, who he could see leaning against a wall. She was holding Daniel in her arms, sobbing, with the pushchair next to her. Both Tina and Crane were attracting strange looks from people passing by, but all of them were too intent on either getting into the store to spend their money on stuff they didn't really need, or getting their loaded trolleys over to their cars before anyone pinched what they'd just bought. So even though Crane and Tina were creating a spectacle, nobody interfered.

Before he said anything, Crane wrapped his arms around both his wife and child. Tina was red faced and her hair was damp with sweat. She had on a coat she owned before she had the baby, that didn't fit her anymore, over jeans and a baggy jumper.

"Are you alright?" he whispered in Tina's ear.

She managed to nod against his shoulder.

"Is Daniel alright?"

She moved a little so he could see the baby and whispered back, "Yes, he's fine."

"Okay, do you think you can walk to the car? It's

just over there," he inclined his head.

Again Tina nodded and Crane saw that at least her tears were drying up.

As he stepped back, he moved to take Daniel out of Tina's arms but she screamed, "No, no! Leave him alone!"

So Crane did as he was asked, collecting the pushchair instead. When they reached the car, Tina still wouldn't let go of Daniel, so he put her in the back seat with Daniel in her arms and stowed the pushchair in the boot, keeping his fingers crossed all the way home that they didn't pass a police car and get stopped for not using a baby seat.

After parking on the drive, he went around the car and opened the door for Tina, who still wouldn't let him take the child from her. They went into the house and Crane had no choice but to seat them both on the settee. After making some tea and warming a bottle for Daniel, he finally managed to persuade Tina to take their coats off.

As she was feeding Daniel, she told Crane what happened.

"I left him in Tesco. Can you believe that? My own baby! I paid for my shopping and then just walked away with the carrier bag, leaving him strapped in the pushchair at the check-out. I only realised what I'd done when I got to the front door of the store and someone came running after me asking if I'd left my baby behind."

"What were you thinking of?" Crane asked.

"You, well, us. I couldn't get what happened last night out of my head. I still feel I'm such a failure at this mothering and housewife bit. Fancy you coming home after a long day at work and there was no meal and I'm asleep. It's not right. It's my fault. I don't know what to do."

Tina broke down in tears once again, but this time let Crane take the dozing baby. He winded Daniel and then went upstairs and put him in his cot. Whilst there, he pulled out his mobile phone and called Tina's mother.

Back at Tina's side he said, "I've called your mother, love. Daniel's asleep, so why don't you put your feet up on the settee and see if you can get some sleep as well. Your Mum has a key to let herself in, so don't worry about that and then there'll be someone here when you wake up. I'm sorry, but I've got to go back to work."

Tina nodded her agreement and lay on the settee. Moments later she was fast asleep. Crane looked at her red rimmed eyes and ravaged face and started to formulate a plan.

A quick check on the internet back in his office was all it took to help Crane understand that his wife wasn't going nuts - it was more than likely she was suffering from post natal depression. Eventually he managed to speak to their family doctor, who confirmed two vital points. Firstly Tina needed to understand that seeking help for postnatal depression did not mean that she was a bad mother or unable to cope. In fact it was these very feelings that were a symptom of the illness, along with her tiredness and inability to look after herself properly. Secondly, and equally important as far as Crane was concerned, post natal depression needed to be properly treated and wasn't something she could just snap out of. So it was vitally important that Crane understood Tina needed help and encouragement for the moment, not criticism and sarcasm.

As a result, he'd talked to friends and family and now had a rota of helpers for Tina. He looked at the timetable on his desk, which he'd hastily sketched out. He'd managed to elicit help from Tina's mum Carol, Derek Anderson's wife Jean, a couple of the mums in his street and even Kim, who wanted to be involved to take her mind off her own problems.

Crane had to admit his own failings in this area. He just didn't do emotion. He suppressed his emotions so much whilst on duty, that he found it difficult to be 'a civvy' when around the family. Since Daniel had been born he had tried harder than ever and acknowledged he loved Tim and Daniel deeply. He'd fight to the death for them, equalling his sense of duty and commitment to the army. But he just didn't know what to say to Tina when she fell apart, when she wanted to talk about her feelings of guilt and failure. It seemed to him his words of support came out as platitudes.

So he had come to a realistic decision. Tina needed the help of people who really understood post natal depression and his rota would ensure she was in the company of her women friends during the day and at night if necessary, when he was working. He'd do what he does best. Organise, co-ordinate and provide practical back-up. In other words, he'd employ his skills as a soldier to best help his family.

Satisfied with his work for the day, he was leaving the office, clutching his precious timetable when his telephone rang.

Chapter 28

"What?" Crane growled into the telephone.

"It's Staff Sgt Jones, sir." Jones used his own formal title and finished with 'sir' Crane noted. His voice must have really conveyed his annoyance and the thought made him smile.

"This better be good, Staff, I'm just leaving to go home."

"Oh it is, sir. We've just caught Fitch 'in the act' so to speak, in Private Turner's room in the single men's barracks."

"Bloody hell, I'll bet that was a sight for sore eyes, well done, Staff."

Crane couldn't believe their good luck.

"Yes, well, Fitch is claiming it was consensual. But I'm a witness to, well, his, um, rape of Turner."

"Okay, who is where and who is with them?"

"Fitch is locked up in the Guard Room. No visitors allowed. I'm just leaving him to think about the predicament he's in. Private Turner is with the duty doctor at the moment, having a rape kit examination done."

"Good. Get Billy to do forensics on the room right

away and then keep Turner company and take his statement. I think Billy is the person Turner trusts most, so he should be the one to take his statement. He might not speak freely to anyone else."

"Very well, sir. Are you coming over?"

"No. It's not that I don't want to, but tonight I'm needed at home. Tina's had a, um, bad day. Tell Billy to leave Turner's statement in my office. I'll read it first thing in the morning and then we can interview Fitch afterwards."

Tina had somehow lost the shopping she bought, before the fiasco in Tesco. So they were reduced to a plate of pasta covered in a bolognaise sauce for their evening meal. Crane insisted it was one of the best things he had ever eaten and cleared his plate, whilst Tina pushed the pasta around hers, trying to look as though she was eating it. Crane couldn't watch her not eating anymore, so went to the sink, to wash the dishes from their meagre meal.

"I'm sorry, Tom," she mumbled to Crane's back. As he turned around he saw exhaustion had etched new lines on her face and her normally long sleek dark hair was tied back, to try and hide the fact it needed washing. She was still dressed in the jeans and baggy jumper she was wearing when he collected her from Tesco earlier in the day.

Drying his hands on a towel, he pulled out a chair and sat back at the table.

Grasping one of her hands he said, "Tina, please stop apologising."

But his words didn't seem to offer her any comfort, as her tears spilled into the mug she was holding up to her face.

"I never thought I'd be this useless," she said hiccupping back sobs. "It's much harder than working in the bank. I just can't seem to cope at all."

Crane got up and moved his chair so he could sit next to her and put his arm around her, drawing her close. Taking a deep breath Crane decided to embark on the conversation he'd been waiting to have since he got home. It was now or never, he thought.

"Tina, love, I don't think you're very well."

"I think you're right," she agreed in a small voice, "but I don't know what to do about it."

"Well, I think I do. Will you let me help you?"

"Help me? I'm not sure anyone can. I just can't seem to shake off this tiredness and guilt. And the more you help around the house and with Daniel, the worse I feel."

"That's not exactly what I meant, Tina," he said and went on to relay his conversation with their doctor.

To start with Tina stiffened at the thought that she needed to go and see a doctor, especially when Crane uttered the words 'post natal depression'. But as he explained, she gradually relaxed against him. The first thing he stressed was that having this type of depression didn't mean Tina was a bad mother, or that she was unable to cope.

He then said, "The GP said to ask you two questions. This is the first one: during the past month, have you often been bothered by feeling down, depressed or hopeless?"

Crane knew the answer to this question, but realised Tina had to acknowledge it herself. By acknowledging it, she would be more open to help.

As Tina nodded her head in reply, he asked his second question. "Okay love, how about; during the past month have you often been bothered by taking little or no pleasure in doing things that normally made you happy?"

Again the nod.

So it was a very relieved Crane who went to his briefcase in the hall and took out his timetable. He even got a smile from Tina, when he showed her the legion of people who had agreed to come and help on a rota basis.

Chapter 29

Crane closed his eyes and then rubbed them, as though trying to rub away the words contained in Private Turner's statement. What a way to start the day, he thought. He was sickened by both the young lad's experience and the fact that a soldier could do such a thing to anyone. Never mind to a fellow soldier and to someone who Fitch was supposed to be responsible for.

Turning back to the statement in his hands, he read once again how Lance Corporal Fitch had burst into Private Turner's bedroom in the single men's accommodation. He whirled Turner around, pushed him face down on the bed and then forced himself on the hapless young soldier. In the middle of all this, luckily, (or unluckily whichever way you looked at it from Staff Sgt Jones' point of view) Jones arrived at Turner's room. Hearing a scuffle and muffled cries, Jones battered down the door, flew into the room and caught Fitch in flagrante. The statement then relayed the examination Turner was subjected to, when the doctor collected forensic evidence from his body. But more importantly Turner named Fitch, in writing, as the man who had been attacking him systematically over the past few months.

When Billy arrived to do a forensic examination of the room, Turner was discreetly moved into St Omer Village, where he would stay until Crane decided he didn't need him around anymore. He would also be on compassionate leave until the court-martial of Fitch.

Crane knew he has to get used to calling St Omer Barracks, St Omer Village. The concrete tower block called St Omer Barracks was demolished some time ago and rebuilt with modular units. These housed the Olympic and Paralympic athletes during their training preparations for the London 2012 Olympic Games.

The old concrete structure used to house the Army Catering School, where a tribe of Sgt Majors from the Army Catering Corp whipped new chefs into shape. There the recruits undertook a rigorous training programme, ensuring that chefs attached to Regiments were able to cater for hundreds of soldiers, no matter what their location - in barracks, out in the field, or in times of war. Indeed many chefs perished on the Sir Galahad during the Falkland's War, where they were waiting to disembark to provide support for the front line troops.

The other thing St Omer Barracks was famous for was that the chefs there made the cake for Princess Diana's wedding to Prince Charles, together with all the petit fours for the reception.

Turner should be quite comfortable in St Omer Village with all its new facilities. It now boasted The HUB, a dining centre for serving personnel. It also had a convenience store, a licensed bar, an internet café and TV screens showing popular sporting events. Other amenities included The Physical and Recreation

Training Centre (P&RTC) and The Junior Ranks Pub.

Aware that he was procrastinating by thinking about how things used to be on Aldershot Garrison, Crane turned his attention back to the file. Turner's statement was peppered with expletives. The picture emerging was one of a young man who was angry about the attacks. Crane imagined Turner would be relieved it was all over, as he realised Fitch couldn't touch him anymore. Crane thought the anger a bit strange, but to be honest, knew he had no experience of these things and so had no idea how victims would normally react to being repeatedly raped.

He knew that young soldiers, generally speaking, got very angry from time to time, mostly at those in authority. But eventually they learned to cope with constantly being shouted at, from shouted orders or from being given a dressing down. Still, Crane made a note of Turner's anger on the file.

He was still thinking about Turner when he realised his phone was ringing. Thinking it may be Tina, he snatched it up.

"Sir, we're waiting for you in the conference room for the briefing about Saturday night."

"Oh, right, thanks, Billy, I'll be there in a minute."

Crane didn't know if he was pleased the phone call wasn't from Tina, or not. As it wasn't, it meant she was doing alright. But on the other hand, he couldn't wait to hear how she went on at the doctors. Either way, he had work to do, so collecting his files he pushed his domestic problems to the back of his mind and strode out of the door.

Chapter 30

"I can't believe we're doing this, Crane."

"Oh stop moaning, Derek," Crane grinned, as he put his files in front of the seat next to the policeman. Glad the boot was on the other foot for once and it wasn't Anderson telling him to stop moaning. After putting his suit jacket across the back of the chair, Crane moved to the whiteboard and began the briefing.

"First of all, thanks to everyone for coming along and particular thanks to Kim for agreeing to help try and trap her…attacker."

Crane noticed Kim's head was down and she was looking at her hands in her lap. Dressed in civvies, as she was still on compassionate leave, she was sitting next to Padre Symmonds. Crane watched as the Padre touched her arm and she lifted her head to look at him, managing a small smile.

"Staff Sgt Jones, you first please."

Crane dragged his attention away from Kim, determined to get on with the job. He knew this was the best way he could help her, by finding and prosecuting the bastard responsible - even if he was a squaddie.

"Thank you, sir," Jones began. He was dressed in fatigues, standing out in his army uniform, as everyone else at the meeting was dressed in civvies.

"As you know we normally have two jeeps patrolling Aldershot on a Saturday night. This is being increased to four, each with two RMPs in. I can put more on the streets, but I don't want to make our presence too obvious and scare the bugger away, if that's alright with you, sir?"

Crane nodded his agreement and Jones went on to outline the timings and routes the jeeps would take. This information was highlighted with a Power Point presentation, showing maps of Aldershot town centre and the routes the RMPs would take. He also confirmed a group of four RMPs would be dressed in 'civvies' in the pub.

When Jones finished, Crane asked Anderson to take over. He confirmed the presence of extra police on duty patrolling the streets. Also some off-duty policemen had agreed to have a couple of drinks in The Goose as a favour to him, popping in at various times during the evening.

"The main concern I have at this moment," Anderson continued, "is that our, or rather Sgt Major Crane's suspect, Yasin Whadi, may have become so frightened by the vigorous interviewing he's been subjected to, that he deliberately won't be on the prowl on Saturday night."

"I have to disagree there, Derek," Crane said. "I think he's an arrogant little shit. The type who doesn't thinks he can't get caught. He probably thinks he can get one over on us. No, I reckon we've made sure he'll be there. He'll want to prove that he can do what he likes, right under our noses."

"Fair enough," Anderson conceded. "Only time will tell if you're right, Crane."

Anderson, having finished his briefing, returned to his seat around the table.

It was then Billy's turn. He confirmed he had his 'penguin suit' at the ready and would be on the door with the regular bouncers from 19:00 hours. Should any one ask why there was an extra body helping out, the cover story would be that he was a trainee gaining valuable work experience. Crane knew Billy would take some stick for that from the rest of SIB and smiled at the prospect.

Kim and the Padre confirmed they would arrive around 21:00 hours. Kim explained that she couldn't do this on her own, which was why she'd asked the Padre to be her 'date' for the night. Crane wondered out loud if this might make the man stalking Kim even angrier, but Anderson disagreed. His opinion was that this could be a good thing. If the suspect was angry he may make a mistake and therefore become more obvious and easier to identify and restrain.

As the meeting broke up, Crane wandered over to Kim.

"How are you doing?" he asked.

"Holding up, sir, thank you."

"This is a very brave thing you're doing, you know, Kim."

"Is it sir? It doesn't feel it."

"Well it is. It means you're standing up to your attacker. Not letting him get away with it. So take a deep breath and hold your head up. Come on, you can do it."

Crane was pleased to see Kim straighten her shoulders and make an attempt to stand tall. He realised she has a long way to go yet, but hoped his plan would give her some self esteem and self confidence back and give her a sense of taking back control of her life.

As Crane left the building, he paused for a cigarette in the car park and recognised the similarities in the two cases of rape he was investigating. Similarities for the victims, that was. Both had been subjected to a horrific attack. Both of them had to bear the ignominy of an intimate examination. They were both dealing with the prejudice that comes with being raped. Other people taking the view that it was 'the victim's fault' somehow. Kim's fault for wearing provocative clothes, or Turner's for displaying homosexual tendencies. Crane had to admit to himself that before these cases, that was his attitude. Very much a case of 'well they asked for it'. But now he knew better, had learned that lesson, but winced as he thought of the trauma the victims had gone through in order for him to do so.

As he ground out his cigarette under foot, he once more pushed his worries that someone could get hurt on Saturday night to the back of his mind and walked into Provost Barracks to interview Fitch.

A letter to Billy

Dear Billy

I constantly question myself. Is this all my fault? Do I have homosexual tendencies that I unconsciously use to attract other men? Will I ever be able to have a normal heterosexual relationship after this is over, or am I really a closet homosexual? I can't get past the things he made me do, not only to him but to myself. He made me shave down there, because he preferred me that way. A small matter, you may say, but to me it was another form of control. Of making sure he was in my mind every time I went to the toilet, changed my clothes or took a shower.

I used to find it easy to get a girlfriend or just a one night stand when I wanted sex. I used to enjoy female company. Enjoyed the flirting, the banter and then the thrill of a new relationship. But now I fear that is all gone. I fear I'll never be able to get past what this bastard has done to me. He's not only ruined my army life, he's ruined my sex life as well.

So make sure you lock him up and throw away the key, as they say. He needs to pay for the rest of his life for what he's done to me. I know I will.

Chapter 31

There were three of them in the interview room in Provost Barracks; Crane, Billy and Lance Corporal Fitch. A blank room, with nothing to catch the eye, nothing to detract from the interview about to take place. As he looked Fitch over, Crane was surprised by the Lance Corporal's appearance, half expecting a bull of a man, someone big enough to physically overpower Seb Turner. Instead he saw a gangly youth leaning back in his chair, all arms and legs and sharp points.

"Have you forgotten something, Lance Corporal?" Crane barked.

Fitch took his time getting off the chair and standing to attention.

"I should bloody well think so."

But instead of an apology, all Crane gets was a barely concealed sneer.

"Right, sit down."

Crane indicated the chair Fitch had just vacated and then sat down himself. He didn't take off his suit jacket and neither did Billy. Crane wanting this interview to be as formal as possible. He took his time opening his file, glancing at it, then silently studying Fitch. Billy, equally silent, moved to sit next to Crane. But Fitch seemed unmoved, and simply stared back.

"So, Lance Corporal, I understand you know Private Sebastian Turner?"

"Yes, sir."

"How do you know him?

"He's in my Unit, sir."

"I know that, Lance Corporal. Would you say you have a more personal relationship with him?"

"No comment, sir."

"No comment, Lance Corporal?"

Billy took a photograph out of the file in front of Crane.

"That's an unusual answer, at least judging by this photograph."

Billy turned one of the more graphic photographs of Fitch in Seb Turner's room, to face him.

Crane noticed Fitch briefly close his eyes before he said, "No comment, sir."

"According to Staff Sgt Jones of the Royal Military Police, it seems you have a rather intimate relationship with Turner. At least from what he saw with his own eyes and from what you said to him. What did Fitch here say, Billy?" asked Crane.

Billy picked up Staff Sgt Jones' statement and read: "I've done nothing wrong. It was consensual. We've been having a relationship for some time now."

"Is that correct, Fitch? Did you say that to Staff Sgt Jones?" asked Crane.

This time Fitch didn't even manage a, 'no comment'.

"Are you calling my Staff Sgt a liar, Lance Corporal? I certainly hope not because if you are that'll be another charge to add to the list."

"The list, sir, what list?"

"Let me see."

Crane made a play of looking in the file for the right piece of paper. He held it up and said, "The rape of Private Turner, assault upon the person of the said Private, breaking and entering Private Turner's room with intent to assault…need I go on?"

"No, sir."

"Excellent, Fitch," Crane said, putting down the blank piece of paper he was reading from. "Let's start again. Were you having an intimate relationship with Private Turner?"

"Yes, sir, but it was consensual," the sneer briefly returned.

But it disappeared again when Crane said, "So, do you deny raping Private Turner?"

"Yes, sir."

"Do you deny assaulting Private Turner?" Billy asked.

"Yes, sir," Fitch turned his head to address Billy.

"What about breaking and entering Turner's room. Do you deny that as well?"

"Sir." Fitch was looking down at the table and managed a nod.

"Oh dear," Crane said. "In that case you've got a bit of a problem, Fitch. Because we've got the evidence to prove you did all those things and you haven't got any to prove you didn't."

"It was consensual, sir," Fitch repeated his mantra.

"Well, lad, you might say that, but God knows how your brief's going to persuade a court-martial to believe you. Charge him, Billy," Crane said and left the room.

"What do you think, Jones?"

Crane and Jones were standing in the cold outside

the barracks, having a quick cigarette. Whilst Crane realised he should give up smoking, he welcomed the time he spent in contemplation in the car park, even though he sometimes stood in a biting wind, as he was now.

"Little shit," said Jones, as he exhaled his cigarette smoke.

"Actually, rather a tall little shit, wouldn't you say? Not exactly the physique I was expecting. He towered over me."

"No, he's not what I expected either," agreed Jones. "I reckon he's done a lot of his bullying by pulling rank. Frightening the poor sod Turner into going along with it. Making sure he didn't say anything by threatening him. Maybe he was picking on him in front of the other lads. That would've helped to isolate Turner and made him more reliant on Fitch. Perhaps Turner was hoping that if he didn't report the bullying, Fitch would stop undermining and humiliating him."

"That's a good point, Staff. I'll get Billy to get another statement from Turner about that. We'll also interview the other soldiers in the Unit. See if they witnessed Fitch bullying Turner. I think the lawyers will want that sort of stuff. They'll want to show bullying and assault over a period of time if they can."

Chapter 32

The thumping beat of the music emanating from three different pubs within a few yards of each other was giving Crane a headache. He was lurking in the entrance to the shopping centre along Victoria Road. Opposite them was The Queens Head (or the Hogs Head as people called it) and a few yards down the road past The Goose was Yates. The Goose was located on the corner of Victoria Road and Wellington Street. Crane wished he could get closer to the pub. The corner opposite The Goose would have been good, but there was more of a chance of a suspect seeing them there. Crane was dressed casually in cargo pants and polo shirt, with a large jacket on, in an attempt to cut out the cold. As he saw young girls passing him, barely dressed, he wondered how they coped with the low temperature. Or was his age showing? No one else seemed to have coats on apart from him and Anderson.

They were using radios to keep in touch, not wanting to wear ear pieces, which would raise a few eye brows. So far it had been very quiet, no one of any note passing through the doors of the pub and definitely no sign of Yasin Whadi. Billy had pulled a couple of suspicious looking blond-haired and dark-haired lads to one side on the pretext of checking their IDs. He'd taken a note of their details as a precaution. Inside The Goose at the moment were a couple of RMPs and a couple of off-duty policemen.

Crane heard two clicks on his radio, pulled it from his pocket and turned his back on the street.

"Yes, Billy."

"Kim's just walking up Victoria Street towards The Goose, sir."

Crane put the radio back in his pocket and motioned to Anderson. Together they strolled down the road, trying to blend in and failing miserably. As they walked up to The Goose they saw Kim and Padre Symmonds at the entrance. Kim had done her best to look normal, dressed in a little black dress, her features emphasised by makeup. The Padre had also made an effort, wearing an open necked shirt and chinos. Crane couldn't help thinking he didn't look right without his dog collar.

As he walked past the pub, Crane managed to catch Kim's eye and give her an encouraging smile, which she returned by raising her eyebrows. Crane noted that the Padre was oblivious to everyone else apart from Kim and was holding her decorously by the elbow. As they walked into the pub, Crane gave three clicks on his radio, the sign that Kim had arrived. Anderson and Crane then turn away, walking back past The Goose, towards their allotted position.

"Fuck this," Crane suddenly said. "I can't do this waiting outside shit. I'm going in," and he shrugged off his coat, thrust it at Derek and walked back to the pub.

Billy's eyes widened at the sight of Crane approaching him, but as he saw Crane's glare he said and did nothing.

Once inside, Crane could understand why no one was wearing a coat. The heat from all the bodies squashed inside had raised the temperature to sweating point. He pushed his way around the bar until he had Kim in his line of sight. Crane stood by a pillar which had a conveniently placed ledge around it for drinks. He pulled a half drunk pint that someone had left towards him, raising the glass to his lips every now and then, but not drinking from it.

Kim had managed to grab a small table and as Crane watched, the Padre returned from the bar with a glass of wine for Kim and a bottle of beer for himself. The Padre sat protectively close to Kim and they both scanned the crowd. Every so often Symmonds pointed someone out, but each time Kim shook her head.

As the time passed and Kim and the Padre nursed their drinks, it was becoming clear that either the attacker wasn't coming, or he had seen that Kim wasn't on her own and so wouldn't make a move. The two RMP lads had worked their way around the bar and were standing within striking distance of Kim and the Padre.

Crane scanned the crowd for anyone looking agitated, or paying too much attention to Kim. But most of the young men were too busy looking at the available girls. The ones provocatively dressed and without an escort. Which, let's face it, was most of the pub. Why else come here if you're not available?

After a couple of hours of nothing but music played too loudly and too many people crammed into too small a space, Kim looked at Crane, then her watch, then back at Crane. After nodding his agreement, Kim and the Padre pushed their drinks away and made to leave. Crane followed them out and stopped at the door to talk to Billy.

"Here's your coat, sir," Billy said, grabbing it off the floor behind him. "DI Anderson said to say he'll see you later at the police station."

"I bet he said more than that," laughed Crane.

"Well, sir, he did. But most of it isn't repeatable."

Chapter 33

I saw you, you bitch. Did you think I wouldn't recognise all your army friends? There to protect you were they? Protect you from me? But they didn't see me, did they? No, but I saw them. Outsmarted them. Out foxed them. Blended into the crowd.

And who was that wimp with you anyway? Call himself a man does he? A bit too meek and mild if you ask me. How could you even stand talking to him, never mind letting him touch you and at one point put his arm around you?

No, Kim, what you need is a real man. What you need is a real man like me!
Strong, brave and loyal.
Have you forgotten already what a good time we had that night?
I haven't. So, if you won't come to me, then I will have to come to you.
I'll find a way.

Sitting at the kitchen table, Crane picked up the note with gloved hands and put it in an evidence envelope.

"This came in the post this morning you say?"

"Yes, sir. I'm sorry but Mum and I touched the note and the envelope before we realised what it was," replied Kim.

Crane was glad to see Kim was much calmer this time, after receiving yet another letter from her stalker. Her reaction was nothing compared to when she received the others. It looked like her chats with the Padre were working. But Crane would neither ask about, nor comment on, what seemed to be a developing relationship. She was also looking better in herself. Today she was dressed in smart trousers and a blouse and was beginning to get back that look - the look of a soldier clearly dressed in civvies.

"That's okay, Kim, it's understandable. Still, I'll get it checked for finger prints anyway. Although I doubt there'll be any. There hasn't been before. Thanks for going to The Goose on Saturday as well, Kim, even though it came to nothing."

As the kettle boiled Kim got out of her chair to make the coffee.

"Well we know why now, sir, don't we," she said returning to the table with two mugs of coffee in her hand. "He recognised someone. I wonder who?"

"Thanks for the coffee," Crane said, blowing on the top before he took a sip. "It's difficult to say," he continued. "There were so many squaddies in the pub that night, apart from us, that it could have been anybody."

"Still, it does seem to point to the fact that he really is in the army if he recognised someone."

"I suppose so, Kim. But it's difficult to be confident

of that as so many of the lads are regulars at The Goose. It stands to reason he knows, or at least recognises, some of them."

"Um, sir, I was just wondering…."

"Wondering what, Kim?"

"The threat at the end of the letter, 'I'll find a way'. How serious is that, do you think?"

"Serious enough for me to ask you to stay somewhere else. I don't think you're safe here with your mum. I'd say the threat level is escalating. I'd be happier if you were somewhere else, maybe somewhere on the Garrison? What do you think?"

"I don't want to run away, sir," Kim shook her head. Her long blond hair was tied up in a ponytail and swung from side to side as she moved her head. "I'm fed up of that. I'm starting to feel stronger, both physically and mentally. I don't want this bastard to make me frightened to go out, or to be alone."

"That's good, Kim, but you also need to be sensible."

Crane's lecture was interrupted, firstly by a knock on the front door and secondly by the Padre walking into the kitchen.

"Hello, Kim. Oh, hello, Crane. Sorry, am I interrupting something?"

"Not at all, sir," Crane said standing and shaking the Padre's hand. "In fact you could help me. I'm trying to persuade Kim here to move to somewhere safer, perhaps onto the Garrison."

"Why what's happened?"

"This arrived this morning."

Crane handed the note in its protective cover to the Padre, who blanched as he read the implied threat contained in it and he sat down at the kitchen table next to Kim. Crane returned to his seat.

"Oh, I see, Crane. Well, I think you may be right. What do you think, Kim?"

"I don't want to be bullied by this man and forced to move out. I've already had to move out of my flat. I thought I'd be safe here with mum, but now it seems I'm not."

Kim was close to tears, despite her earlier determination and claims that she was getting stronger.

"I've got a possible solution," said Captain Symmonds. "You could move in with me, purely on a temporary basis, of course. But I do live on the Garrison and I've got that big house I rattle around in. I know it's not usual practice for a sergeant to associate with a captain, but I think this situation calls for a little, shall we say, bending of the rules. And Kim will be staying in a separate bedroom, of course."

The Captain's little speech came out all in a rush, making Crane smile to himself and Kim blush.

"Well, what do you say, Kim? It's up to you. Are you going to accept the Captain's proposal?" Crane's eyes widened as he teased her.

Before Kim could reply, Crane's mobile rang. "Crane," he answered.

"Sir," said Billy, "I'm over with DI Anderson. The DNA results have just come back on the black hair found on Madison's body. You need to see this."

"Stay there," Crane said. "I'm on my way."

Chapter 34

A stunned Crane sat down on the chair Billy had just cleared for him in DI Anderson's office in Aldershot Police Station. The three of them were sat around the DI's desk.

"They don't match," Crane said for third time. "It's not Yasin Whadi's hair."

"Yes, so you keep saying, Crane. Now do you want to hear the rest?"

"There's more? Good news or bad news?" Crane fingered the scar underneath his beard.

"Well, it depends on which way you look at it. Bad news for me, I guess and good news for you, as we've found a DNA match. But, as you've just said several times, it's not your soldier, it's a local man. He's got a record, which is why we had his DNA. So it reverts from being your case back to mine, as the suspect this time is a civvy."

Anderson handed Crane a buff folder.

Crane read in the file that Albert Watkins was a local man well known to the police. He was arrested several times as a teenager for minor public order and shoplifting offences. As was the norm, unfortunately, instead of getting his act together and doing something with his life, Watkins progressed to burglary, stealing cars, and more interestingly, violent assault charges. Unfortunately the local police hadn't had much evidence against Watkins for many of the offences, so most of the time he'd got away with it.

As far as Crane could see, there were a couple of points which helped build a case against Watkins, apart from the DNA. One was that he had a job as a delivery van driver, so he was a white van man. And secondly, the fact that he was built like a brick shithouse, all muscles and short cropped hair. Crane could see how he could be mistaken for a squaddie from his looks alone.

"Well, it could be him for the local attacks, but I still fancy Whadi for the others," was Crane's opinion.

"Give Whadi a break, Crane. Don't you ever give up?"

"No." Crane emphasised his point by slamming the file on Watkins on Anderson's desk, making Billy jump. "He's still dodgy if you ask me."

"Well I'm not." Anderson picked up his cup of tea. "Whadi is all yours as he's in the army. My focus now is gathering evidence on Watkins."

"With me in tow, don't forget, Derek."

"And what if I say no, Crane?"

"Then I'll take no notice and follow you around anyway."

Anderson had no choice but to laugh. "Alright, Crane. Here, you better have a cake and a cup of tea while we wait for Watkins to be brought in."

So Crane did just that, sending Billy back to Provost Barracks.

Crane was right in his assessment of Watkins. As he and Anderson walked into the interview room, Watkins rose from his chair and towered over the two men.

"Sit down, Albert. Stop making a tit of yourself, trying to be macho and intimidating. You really should know better."

"Sorry, Mr Anderson."

"DI Anderson to you."

"Who's this bloke then," Watkins ignored the rebuke and peered closely at Crane.

"Army."

"Oh, Special Branch innit?"

"No, Albert, that's the spooks. Sgt Major Crane here is Special Investigations Branch. SIB to you and me."

"Yeah, right, I've heard about you lot. Right hard, so I hear."

"Yes, well, your thoughts on the SIB are neither here nor there, so stop twittering on and listen to me for a change."

"Right you are, Guv. What can I do for you?" Albert turned his attention back to DI Anderson.

Throughout this exchange Crane tried hard not to sit there with his mouth open. It became clear as soon as Watkins began to speak that he may look like a squaddie but he certainly wasn't army material. Nor could Crane see him as rapist material. Watkins seemed too much of a gentle giant. Still, Crane decided to keep an open mind as he relaxed back against his chair, crossing his legs, enjoying the pantomime being played out before him.

"Would you mind telling me where you were last Saturday night, Albert?"

"Don't rightly know, Mr Anderson."

"What about the previous two Saturdays?"

"Not really sure about those nights either."

"Why not?"

"Because that's the night I tend to get plastered, Mr Anderson. And once I get plastered the old memory goes you know? You see I drive during the week, so I have to be good with the old pop, if you know what I mean. But Saturday night, I don't have to worry, see, because I don't have work the next day."

"Where do you drink?" Crane had had enough of this nonsense and decided to join in.

"Normally at the bar, don't like sitting down, a bit poncy if you ask me."

"No. I. Mean. Which. Pub?" Oh dear God save me, thought Crane, trying hard not to put his head in his hands.

"Here and there, Guv. Wherever the fancy, or the lads, take me, I suppose."

"Do you drink in The Goose?" Anderson asked.

"The Goose?"

"Yes, The Goose," Crane confirmed.

"Why ever would I do that? It's full of your lot," Watkins said, looking at Crane.

"I'll tell you what, Albert, why don't you just wait here while Sgt Major Crane and I just go and check on something?"

"If you say so, Mr Anderson. Any chance of a cup of tea while I'm waiting?"

Crane and Anderson staggered out of the room, bursting out laughing as they closed the door behind them.

"In the words of the great John McEnroe 'you cannot be serious'," Crane quipped.

"Don't start or we'll never stop laughing," said Anderson wiping tears from his eyes.

"Dear God, Derek, where ever did you find him?" Crane took deep breaths to calm himself down. "Surely he can't have done it. Anyway I can't see the uptight, straight laced, hard working Kim finding him attractive, can you?"

"No, can't say as I do, Crane and he said he doesn't go in The Goose. But he's a delivery driver, so he could have done the other rapes if his routes take him there. Plus you can't get away from the fact that a hair with his DNA was found on the body of one of the victims."

That sobered Crane up.

"No, you're right about the hair, Derek. I wonder how that happened."

Chapter 35

Crane was standing at his white boards, as Billy came up and handed him a coffee.

"Any new insights, sir?"

"Not so as you'd notice, Billy, but while you're here, let's have a look at each case in turn."

"Now how did I know you were going to say that, boss?"

"Because it's what we do, Billy. We look at the evidence, discuss it, speculate and then follow up on that speculation to see if the lead goes anywhere. Right, update me on Lance Corporal Fitch."

"Well, sir, nothing new on that one really, it's just about wrapped up. I went to see Private Turner and took another statement about Fitch's behaviour as you suggested. You were right; the bullying had been going on for a long time. In fact it started before the physical attacks. By the time Fitch was ready to rape him, Turner had been brow beaten into believing he was worthless anyway. His self esteem was non-existent and he was mentally unable to protest about the rape, never mind physically."

"I can't believe no one noticed," Crane said after

taking a sip of his coffee. "What about the other lads in the Unit?"

"The RMP have taken statements from them and the consensus seems to be that they made sure they didn't get on the wrong side of Fitch. Some of them were actually glad Turner was the victim, because it could just as easily have been them. Also Fitch was quite subtle; he left the really nasty remarks and punishments for when he was on his own with Turner. That way no one really understood how bad the bullying was."

"It's remarkable that Private Turner was brave enough to report it at all. You did a good job there, Billy, gaining his trust and helping him through the reporting procedure."

"Thanks, sir. I'm pretty pleased with that myself. Just shows I'm not all brawn and no brains, eh, boss?"

That made Crane smile but he declined to comment and turned to the next board.

"Right, Becca Henderson. Still no forensics?"

"No, boss," Billy said, sitting down on the corner of a desk. "Not a bloody thing. Stuff taken from her flat and from her body has gone through the lab and there's nothing."

"So we're only left with the witness statements?"

"Yes, sir, that's about it. A description of a tall blond squaddie, from Becca's friend and from the bartender. The one you call 'blond streak'."

But Crane was too involved with his white boards to raise a smile. "Next in line is Kim's board. This time the attacker is described as tall and dark," he said.

"Yes, sir, by both Kim and a couple of her girl friends. Also he's still around as he's stalking her."

Billy nodded at copies of the notes pinned next to

photographs of Kim and her small apartment.

"Yes, so that case could be Yasin, but the blond cases can't be him. But I still fancy him for those unsolved cases you found in other Garrison towns as well."

Crane decided to sit down and pulled up a chair, sitting on it backwards and leaning on the upright.

"I'm still waiting for copies of the files to come through. At the moment, though, it could just be coincidence, sir." As Crane glared at him, Billy quickly said, "Or maybe not," and looked down at his drink.

"Let me know when you've got the files and looked through them."

"Sir." Billy agreed.

"So, the next one is Madison. Yet again dark-haired suspect and this time we have a hair."

"But it matches Watkins, sir and even you don't think it's him."

"No, I don't. But I'm going to get Kim to do an identification parade anyway. Arrange it with DI Anderson will you?"

"Yes, sir."

"Billy?"

"Sir?"

"How are you remembering these instructions?"

"Remembering, sir?"

"Yes, where's your bloody note book!"

"Oh, shit, sorry, boss. I'm used to Kim taking notes for me."

"Yes, well, we're used to Kim doing a lot of things around the office that aren't getting done as well as usual. Let's just hope she's back with us soon."

As Crane was speaking, Billy was scrabbling for his notebook and Crane gave him a minute to make sure he had everything written down.

"Any forensics back from Madison's flat?"

"Not yet, boss. I'll chase up the lab."

Crane was pleased to see Billy making a note of that instruction.

"Right, now the last two boards. We'll do Summer in a moment, firstly Fitch and Turner, what's happening there?"

"All the paperwork has gone through the channels and is with the Military Justice System. We're just waiting for a hearing date."

"Excellent, at least one case has gone smoothly."

"Which case is that, sir?"

Crane and Billy whirled round at the sound of Kim's voice.

"Kim! Um, how are you? Good to see you. Billy get Kim a chair."

Billy pulled a chair away from the conference table, with all the flourish of a magician.

"There you are milady," he said with a grin.

"Bugger off, Williams," Kim grinned back and remained standing.

"Good idea that, Kim. Billy, bugger off and get us some drinks. It's good to see you, Kim. How are you feeling?"

Crane moved to stand in front of the board detailing Kim's attack, to spare her, but he wasn't quick enough.

"Alright, sir, considering." But Kim seemed more interested in where Crane was standing, than in his questions. "Who's that, sir?"

"Who's who?"

"The photograph on my board, sir. It's alright, you know. I've come into the office to see how I feel about being back. Captain Symmonds came with me."

"Oh, sorry, sir didn't see you back there." Crane nodded in Symmonds direction.

Captain Symmonds moved to stand protectively next to Kim.

"So, what photograph are you hiding, then, Sgt Major?" he asked.

Crane realised he couldn't pretend he didn't know what they were talking about, so moved away from the board where he was trying to cover up a picture of Watkins.

"This is the picture of the man whose hair was found on Madison's body."

"So why is it on my board?"

As Kim seemed determined to talk about the case, Crane thought it may do her good. So he went on to explain that he had put the picture of Watkins on her board as he wanted to do an identification parade, to see if she recognised him.

Kim moved to stand in front of the photograph.

"Can't say as I do, sir, at least not from the photograph."

Crane tried to hide his disappointment.

"Oh well, perhaps it might be better when you see him in an ID parade."

"Can we still do one, sir? I've seen his photo."

"Seen what photo?" Billy had returned with refreshments and passed mugs of tea around.

"The photo of this bloke, Watkins," Crane said.

"Oh, him, yeah, fancy finding a longish black hair of his on Madison's body. Seems a bit odd that, especially as he's got a buzz hair cut."

Kim moved and took the photo off the board, looking closely at it.

"When was this taken, sir?"

"I'm not sure. It's a police photo taken when he was arrested at some time or other."

"Well if he's got a buzz cut now, this must be an old photo."

"What makes you say that?"

"Because I think he has long hair that's scraped back. You can't really see any of it, so at first glance he could have a short haircut, as it's only a face-on picture. Look, sir."

Kim held the photograph next to her face, where she had her long blond hair scraped off her face.

"See what I mean? If you look at me straight on you can't see my hair is tied back. It just looks short."

"Bloody hell, you're right, Kim. I wonder when he had it cut." Crane put down his cup. "Right, better get onto DI Anderson, thanks, Kim," and Crane walked off to his own office to make the call.

Chapter 36

DI Anderson thought Crane's question hilarious.

"You want me to ask him when he had his hair cut?" he laughed.

"Yes, Derek. We think at one stage he had long hair and had it cut off. Can you find out if that's true?"

"I can go and ask him. We're still holding him here, pending the background checks."

"Good, wait for me, I'm coming over."

Crane put down the phone, grabbed his jacket and returned to the conference table, to find Kim and Captain Symmonds had gone.

"Is Kim alright?" Crane asked, immediately worried that seeing her incident board could have brought on another flashback.

"Yes, she's fine, boss," replied Billy. "She just said that she didn't want to get in the way."

"Get in the way?"

"Well, she actually said, 'I better be off, Billy, as you'll use my presence as an excuse not to work.'"

Billy looked offended, but Crane thought Kim's assessment was spot on.

"Never mind that, we're off to see DI Anderson,

come on," and Crane swept out of the room, leaving Billy to follow in his wake.

Watkins looked anxious as Crane and Anderson confronted him in an interview room. Crane was all business with his files in front of him on the table. Anderson just looked bemused by the whole hair thing.

"Can't I go, Mr Anderson?" Watkins whined. "I've told you I haven't anything to do with these girls getting hurt."

Crane saw Watkins was looking decidedly fed up and was plonked on his chair like a sack of potatoes.

"Just as soon as we get something cleared up," replied Anderson.

Watkins brightened, sitting up straighter, "What's that then?"

"Your hair, Albert."

"What about it?" asked Watkins, running his hand over his buzz cut.

"Did you have long hair?"

"Oh, yes, now you mention it, Mr Anderson, I did. See, I got it cut for charity, like. Wanted to do a bit of good for a change, so I had it all off."

Watkins looked proud of himself.

"When was that?"

"Oh, must be about three months ago now. A few of us had it done at the same time. It was for a local hospice if I remember rightly. You know them that are dying…"

"Yes, thank you, Albert," cut in Anderson.

"Where did this take place?" Crane got out his notebook.

"Oh, let me think, that barber near the bottom of Victoria Street."

"Right, thank you, Mr Watkins," said Crane and left the room with Anderson following.

"What are you thinking, Crane?"

"It'll all become clear soon enough, be back in a minute."

Crane nodded to Billy and they left the station and made their way to the barbers.

From the outside, the place looked like two different shops, on one side the men's barber and on the other a ladies hairdresser. But on entering the barber's side, Crane saw that in fact it was one huge unit, with a waist high wall separating the two businesses. A girl cutting the hair of a squaddie looked over at them.

"Take a seat," she mumbled. "Giorgio will be out in a minute."

Crane and Billy took a seat and Billy started to thumb through a motor magazine left on the table. But he didn't get very far before a small dark-haired man hurried out to meet them.

"Right, gents, who's first? Hum, you I reckon," he said looking closely at Crane's hair. "Army, right?" and without waiting for an answer went on to say, "Well your hair's a bit too long I'd say and your beard needs a trim."

"Thank you for your interest in my hair, Giorgio is it?"

The barber nodded his assent.

"But I'm not here about a haircut. We're SIB."

Crane and Billy flashed their identifications. Crane watched the barber stiffen and the lad in the chair having his hair done, who was watching them a minute ago, began intently studying his reflection in the mirror.

"Oh, I see. What can I do for you?"

"I understand you cut the hair of Albert Watkins, for a charity stunt."

Billy handed Giorgio the photograph.

"Oh, yes, I remember, about four of them had their hair off at the same time. What I bloody mess it made I can tell you. They all had hair long enough to put in a ponytail. But there's nothing wrong in that, is there?"

"No, sir, nothing at all," said Billy retrieving the photo.

"What did you do with all that hair?" asked Crane.

But Giorgio won't meet his glare and his eyes slid away.

"It's a simple question, sir," added Billy.

"I, um, I um,"

"Come on, Giorgio, we're only interested in the hair. We're investigating a particularly nasty crime, so unless you want to come to the police station and talk to DI Anderson about it, perhaps you better tell me now."

Giorgio's legs gave way and he dropped down onto a sofa covered with red plastic, intended to resemble leather.

Putting his head in his hands, he mumbled, "I sold it."

"Sold it?"

"Yes, I sold it to a wig maker."

"And didn't declare the money, I suppose."

"Yes, I mean no, I…"

"Don't worry, I'm not interested in your tax free money making schemes, just go and get us the details of the wig maker, please."

"Bloody hell, boss," Billy said as Giorgio scurried to his office to get the information, "nice one. Our attacker's been wearing a wig!"

"Yes. It seems he's definitely been wearing a black

one and possibly a blond one as well, which would account for the different descriptions. Let's get the information back to Anderson and he can make enquiries of the wigmaker."

Chapter 37

With the conundrum of the black hair sorted out and in DI Anderson's hands, Crane felt he could concentrate once again on Yasin Whadi, so he was sitting in his office, going through Yasin's records and statements. In an interview room in the Guard House, the young lad was still protesting his innocence, although not as vehemently as he did when he was first interviewed.

Gathering up his papers, Crane decided to go outside and have a cigarette before interviewing Whadi. As he paced up and down the car park outside Provost Barracks, Staff Sgt Jones came out to join him.

"Morning, Jones," called Crane and offered the Staff Sergeant a cigarette.

"Cheers, Crane," Jones bent to light the cigarette. "It's getting bloody cold out here," he complained, stamping his feet. "How are Tina and Daniel?"

"Fine, thanks."

But Crane's face must have belied his words as Jones peered and asked, "Are you sure, Crane?"

"Well, you know, it's always a bit of an upheaval having a new baby in the house, takes time to adjust and all that. He's growing quick, mind," and Crane showed Jones a few photos on his mobile phone, as a way of avoiding any further conversation about the precarious state of his domestic arrangements and Tina's health.

By the end of their cigarettes, they had viewed all the pictures and Crane followed Jones to the Guard House, where Yasin was in an interview room.

"Any particular line of enquiry today, boss?" asked Billy as he joined Crane, looking through the two way glass at the young soldier who had an air of defeat about him. His shoulders were slumped; he was dishevelled and looked pale under his olive hued skin.

"Just follow my lead, Billy. It'll all become clear in due course."

Billy threw Crane a strange look, but didn't speak as they entered the interview room. Yasin turned bloodshot eyes towards Crane, before dropping his head to look at the floor once more.

"Haven't you forgotten something again, soldier?" Crane barked.

"No, sir, I haven't, I just don't seem to have the energy to move. Anyway what are you going to do to me? Put me on report? What difference would that make? I couldn't be in a worse predicament than I am already. I'm being accused of raping and killing girls here in Aldershot and in other Garrison towns."

"No, that's true, I suppose," said Crane pulling out a chair and sitting down. "Particularly as the bloke you're in cahoots with, is getting away with it."

"Bloke? Cahoots? What are you talking about now?"

"Your accomplice, lad. You must have had a partner in all this. Did you two think you could fool us because you're so different? You being dark-haired and dark-skinned and him being blond."

Billy smiled and joined in, "Seems a shame for you to take the fall for all the offences, don't you think, Lance Corporal?"

"Sergeant Williams, is right, son. You're going away for a long time. Stop shielding this other bloke."

"It'll look good with the court-martial and with the Aldershot Police, wouldn't you say, sir?" Billy was clearly enjoying himself.

"I'd say so, Sgt Williams. So, what do you think, Yasin? Are you going to tell us who you're protecting?"

Yasin nodded a small defeated movement.

"Is that a yes?"

"Yes, sir, but it's not a bloke I'm protecting."

"Not a bloke?" Billy asked. "Surely it's not a woman?"

Unbelievably Yasin nodded his head in agreement.

"You mean to tell me a woman has been involved in these vicious attacks? Are you having me on, Lance Corporal?"

Crane had definitely been thrown a curved ball this time.

"No, sir," Yasin lifted his head and looked at Crane. "I'm not having you on and it's not a woman doing the attacking. I'm telling you I've been trying to protect my girlfriend."

"What?" Billy and Crane said together.

"My white girlfriend, sir, I was with her on the nights of the rapes. I was seen with her in The Goose. The blond girl I was talking to. She's my long term girlfriend. We want to get engaged, but…"

"But what, Lance Corporal?" asked Crane although he thought he knew what was coming.

"My family don't know about her. They think I should marry someone from Afghanistan. They're very traditional in their values and their religion. They just wouldn't accept me marrying a white girl. I'm not traditional, or religious and I just want to be allowed to live a normal western way of life. And…" Again Yasin trailed off.

"And?" this time it was Billy prompting.

"And I was afraid they might do something to her if they found out about her. So we are waiting until my next posting. She'll follow me there and we can set up home together. It's just too dangerous for us here in Aldershot, too many of my family live here."

By the end of his story Yasin had tears falling down his face. No wracking sobs, no hitching of his shoulders, just the tears. Crane wasn't sure if Yasin was ashamed of trying to deceive everyone, including Crane and his parents. But one thing was for sure, it was Crane that felt ashamed. Ashamed of letting his unfounded prejudices get in the way of the truth.

Chapter 38

During the past week, there had been no more messages sent to Kim and no further attacks on vulnerable girls from The Goose. However, Crane couldn't shake the feeling that it wasn't the end. They hadn't caught the bastard, and it was clearly not Yasin, so either the rapist had moved on to another town, or was just taking a break. Why he should be taking a break, Crane had no idea, but he wanted to be ready, just in case. Which was why, on yet another Saturday night, Crane and Billy were in Aldershot town centre. It was 23:00 hours and they were sat in Crane's Ford Focus, parked just around the corner from The Goose.

They were cold, miserable and bored. Plus they were freezing their bollocks off, because Crane didn't want to draw attention to their car by running the engine and having the heating on. Billy kept complaining of getting cramp in his legs from being scrunched up in the passenger seat. Crane couldn't do anything about that, though. It wasn't his fault Billy was over six feet tall. He really could do with a cigarette, but wouldn't open the window and have one, because blowing the smoke out of the car, could potentially, draw attention to them.

Crane was just beginning to agree with Billy that their surveillance was a complete waste of time, when his phone rang. It was one of the bouncers on the door at The Goose.

"Some bloke has just left," he told Crane. "He's holding up his girlfriend, who was saying she doesn't feel right. Can't put my finger on it, but it looks wrong somehow. I'd say the bloke was completely sober, but trying to act drunk."

"Describe them," Crane said.

"Tall dark-haired bloke, with small blond-haired woman. She's got a busty top thing on and he's got on dark trousers and white shirt. They're heading your way."

Crane closed the phone without saying good bye and relayed the info to Billy, who got out of the car and walked towards The Goose. Crane watched through the windscreen as Billy suddenly patted his pockets as though he'd forgotten something and began walking back towards the car. Instead of getting in, Billy walked on to the end of the road, towards the public car park.

Just after Billy passed him, Crane saw the man and the girl walking towards the car. He slid down in the seat as they passed and hoped he couldn't be seen in the dark. The man was indeed tall and dark-haired, but it wasn't possible to make out his features in the dim light. He was pulling the girl along, trying to hurry her up. Crane watched through the rear view mirror as they reached the end of the road and disappeared from view. He started the engine in anticipation of Billy identifying a car for them to follow.

Glancing out of his side mirror, Crane saw Billy running towards him and leaned over to open the passenger door.

As Billy slid in he said, "Red BMW Mini just pulled out of the car park, heading down the road towards the station."

"Shit!"

Their car was facing the wrong way, so Crane made the quickest three point turn he'd ever done and raced to the junction, where they needed to turn left to follow the Mini. As he was about to make the turn, a large Aldershot Town Council rubbish lorry pulled up in front of him, completely blocking the road junction.

"Get out of the bloody way," he shouted as he pressed the button to wind his window down.

But the workers cleaning up the litter around the bin they were emptying took no notice of him and ambled off, following in the wake of the large lorry. By the time it had moved out of the way and Crane could turn left, the Mini was at the junction at the bottom of the road, turning right and going out of view.

Crane raced down the road, ignoring the traffic lights which had turned red and slewed right, narrowly missing another car. As they climbed the incline and went around a bend, the Mini was nowhere to be seen. Crane stopped at the junction at the top of the road, looking left and right, but the only signs of life were a couple of taxis.

"Shit."

Crane decided to turn left, away from the town centre, as he thought it the most likely alternative. As Crane drove, Billy scoured the road in front of and behind them and peered down each side turning.

"Sorry, boss, nothing." Billy ran his hand through his hair, smoothing it down after his run back to the car.

"He could be miles away by now," said Crane.

"Those Minis are powerful, especially if it's a Cooper or a Cooper S."

"Or he could have already turned into a driveway, or parked in front of a block of flats. We've no way of knowing." Billy sounded despondent.

Crane and Billy cruised around for another fifteen minutes, without catching sight of the red Mini, before giving up and going home.

The first thing Billy said to Crane as he entered the barracks on Monday morning was, "Anything, boss?"

"No, nothing," replied Crane, who was already at his desk, going through his paperwork, before his briefing with Captain Edwards. For once the heating was working overtime in the barracks and Crane had taken his suit jacket off, which was now hanging over the back of his chair.

"Well that's good," said Billy. "I kept anticipating a call from you all day Sunday, but nothing came. So it looks as if there wasn't anyone raped on Saturday night. Perhaps we got the wrong car."

"Or we got the right one, but because we lost him, another poor girl got attacked."

"We'd have heard something from DI Anderson if that had happened, boss."

"Yes, but only if the girl reported the rape. What if she's too ashamed or frightened? Not everyone reports a rape to the police, you know. I've been reading up on it," continued Crane. "It seems a lot of victims would rather suffer in silence than be subjected to the physical examination, or having to face their attacker in court, where the defence lawyers are only interested in pulling the victim's character apart. Anyway, you only have to look at Seb Turner. Think about how long it took him to pluck up the courage to report Fitch."

"Yes, I suppose you're right, sir. Either that or a victim is lying dead somewhere and no one's found her yet," Billy shivered. "Doesn't bear thinking about," he said as he ambled off. "Do you want coffee, sir?" he called over his shoulder.

"No thanks, Billy. I've got to go and see Captain Edwards."

Crane knew he was in trouble, when Captain Edwards kept him standing to attention in front of the desk, before inviting Crane to sit. He wouldn't have minded but the files he was carrying were bloody heavy. Preparing himself for a bollocking, Crane sat stiffly in his chair, placing his files on the Captain's immaculate desk.

"Ah, Crane," said Captain Edwards, "glad you could make our meeting," looking pointedly at his watch.

"Sorry, sir," Crane apologised, even though, by his own watch which he set by BBC Breakfast television that morning, he was on time. "Here's my latest report, sir." Crane handed over a single sheet of paper.

Captain Edwards took a few moments to read it through, interspersed with a few "Ahs," and "Hums."

Throwing the paper on his desk, and wrinkling his nose, as though it offended his sensibilities, Edwards looked up at Crane.

"So," he started, "if I understand the situation correctly," here we go, thought Crane, recognising the opening words as a prelude to several derogatory comments about his work, "as of this morning, we're nowhere on the rape and murder cases." Edwards maintained his glare.

"Well, sir, I wouldn't put it quite like that."

"How would you put it then, Crane? I'd love to hear your point of view."

Crane opened his mouth to speak, but the Captain carried on.

"Your suspect in the case, Yasin Whadi, has proved to be completely innocent of any involvement with any of the Aldershot cases, or any other Garrison investigation, come to that."

"Sir," was all Crane could manage.

"Also, the hair found on Madison's body appears to have come from a wig made with the hair of a local man, again who is innocent of any involvement in any case whatsoever."

"Sir," Crane responded, thinking that perhaps the Captain should have joined Legal Services. His oratory was a thing of wonder.

"Sgt Weston is being stalked by her attacker and you have *absolutely no idea* who he is."

"Sir," Crane had to admit."

"And, finally, you *lost a possible suspect* on Saturday night. I think that's everything," Edwards once again peered at Crane's report. "In fact, the only thing you've got right is Lance Corporal Fitch's rape of a fellow soldier." Edwards managed a sniff of contempt.

"It would appear so, sir."

"Very well. I welcome your thoughts, in due course, about how you are going to proceed from here on in. Dismissed."

"Thank you, sir," said Crane hurriedly picking up his files and left before Edwards decided to give him a deadline. 'In due course', would do fine for now.

A letter to Billy

Dear Billy,

I suppose I ought to thank you for all the stuff you've done for me up to now. But the truth is I'm not at all sure I am thankful.

To tell you the truth I'm very conscious of the fact that the court-martial is looming. That I'll have to face Fitch in the courtroom and to be honest with you I'm shit scared.

I know I'm doing the right thing by pressing charges, but he's going to be there. In the same room as me. And I know his lawyer is going to try to rip me to shreds. Get me to admit we were in a relationship. Twist my words so they come out all wrong. Make out I'm a bad soldier. Say my reports don't reflect how I acted in the Unit. In fact they're going to throw everything they can at me, aren't they?

It's going to be terrible. What if I have a flashback whilst giving evidence? What will all those high ranking officers think of me? I'm just going to embarrass and humiliate myself. I know I am.

As if I've not been humiliated enough.

Chapter 39

Crane sat in his office, reading the latest forensic reports in the case of the rape of Private Turner. He read, with some satisfaction, that the semen and saliva samples taken from Turner, just after the attack, matched the DNA of Lance Corporal Fitch. Not that there was any doubt, not with Staff Sgt Jones interrupting them, but it was still nice to have. He pulled over his briefcase and put the reports in with the rest of the paperwork on Turner and Fitch. Looking at his watch, he decided it was time to leave to go to the preliminary hearing of the court-martial of Lance Corporal Turner.

The hearing was being held at Bulford Camp in Wiltshire, one of the permanent standing army court locations in the UK, so Crane drove to the nearest junction of the M3, then took the A303 straight through to Bulford, a journey of just over an hour.

Walking into the court complex, he found the officer from the Service Prosecuting Authority who was dealing with the case, one Captain Lisa Nolan. A young, very attractive Captain at that, Crane thought as he tried not to eye her up and down. She did look a bit severe though, Crane decided, a bit like Kim when she was bristling for a fight. Crane hoped he'd see Kim looking just like this again, very soon. Captain Nolan's words brought his attention back to the present.

"Thank you for coming, Sgt Major," she greeted Crane. "Not sure that I'll need you, but you never know. Do you have those reports for me?"

"Yes, ma'am," Crane replied. "The forensic reports confirm the DNA was from Fitch."

Crane put his briefcase on a nearby chair and clicked it open, pulling out a slim buff folder. He handed it over to Captain Nolan who added it to the large pile of papers she was holding in her arms.

"Right, let's go in shall we?"

Crane followed the Captain as she swished into courtroom No 1. All ash furniture and natural sunlight, the courtroom seemed to make a mockery of the severity of the case to be heard in it. He looked around with interest, before the Civilian Judge Advocate and the members of the Board came into the courtroom. Crane was sat behind the Prosecuting Counsel, Captain Nolan and to the side of him was the defence table, where Fitch sat, looking extremely uncomfortable. Crane reckoned he was going to look even more nervous once the judge came in.

A commotion made Crane turn from Fitch and he saw the door behind the top table where the board sit, open.

"All rise," said a disembodied voice.

Crane along with every other person in the courtroom stood briskly to attention, not daring to breathe until the Judge and the Board took their seats, least any movement be construed as a failure to show the court the respect it demanded.

After the formalities of reading out the case and introducing the lawyers took place, Captain Nolan rose.

"At this preliminary hearing, I ask that the court make a date for the case to be heard against Lance Corporal Fitch for the rape and long term bullying of Private Turner, without further delay. The prosecution service is ready to present its case, sir. We can provide witness evidence to the act of rape, DNA evidence to support this act, together with further witness statements from other members of Turner's Unit, testifying to the fact that Lance Corporal Fitch has been systematically bullying Private Turner over a number of months."

Crane saw Fitch sag in his seat a little further, with every blow from Captain Nolan.

"Is there a particular reason for this haste, Captain?"

"Yes, sir. Private Turner and Lance Corporal Fitch's Unit, are due to be shipped out to start their tour of Afghanistan on," Nolan consulted her notes, "the fifteenth of next month, sir. As you can appreciate, it saves the court a great deal of time and trouble if we can hear this witness testimony in person, instead of by video link from Afghanistan, not to mention the disruption it would cause to a Unit on active service, sir."

"I see," the Judge looked at his notes. "What do you say to this, Captain Forbes? Is the defence case ready?"

Captain Forbes jumped to his feet, as if to show he hadn't been caught napping.

"Yes, sir, the defence is ready and we hope the court will look favourably on Lance Corporal Fitch's willingness to have the case tried early." Forbes managed to stand to attention whilst addressing the Judge.

"Yes, yes," the Judge swatted away Forbes' words. "Is the representative from SIB in court, um, Sgt Major Crane?"

The judge peered myopically at his notes, although Crane knew there was nothing wrong with the judge's sight, hearing or intellect.

Crane stood to attention. "Yes, sir."

"Ah, good, morning, Crane, I just want to confirm that SIB is also in a position to proceed. Is there any other line of enquiry you're pursuing against Lance Corporal Fitch?"

"Not at this time, sir."

"Good. Anything else you need to get ready to support your case?"

"No, sir. All the evidence is now collected and in order, sir."

"Very well." The Judge quietly consulted other members of the Board and the court clerk. Raising his head and looking directly at Lance Corporal Fitch, he said, "The date set for hearing is 15th November, in one week's time, court is adjourned until then."

Once again everyone snapped to attention as the Judge and the Board left the courtroom. Lance Corporal Fitch fell back into his seat, the moment the door was closed behind them.

Chapter 40

The following evening, Crane arrived back at Provost Barracks, from yet another meeting with Army Legal Services, to find Billy staring at the white boards. Crane walked up to him, put his briefcase on a desk and looked at his watch to find it was 18:00hours.

"Why are you still here, Billy? Bit late for you isn't it?"

"What? Oh, yes, sir, I'm meeting a mate in the gym at 19:00hours so I thought I'd catch up on stuff."

"Okay," Crane elongated the word, "so how is looking at the white boards catching up on stuff?"

"It's not really is it, sir? I was just trying to see if anything caught my eye."

"In that case, I'll tell you what's caught my eye. Get me a coffee and we'll look at it together."

Crane got the Turner and Fitch files out of his briefcase. He shrugged out of his jacket and slipped it over the back of a nearby chair. Once Billy had placed two coffee mugs on the table, he turned back to the boards.

"Right," Crane explained, "I've been reviewing the evidence to see if there is anything we've missed, or any connections I could make. If you remember we did that on the last big operation, the one when the athletes were here. We looked at each incident in turn and put big arrows to where we could find links between the cases."

"Yes, sir, I remember…"

"Anyway, the thing is, I know we think the rape of Seb Turner and the rape of Kim and the other girls are completely separate cases that just happened to crop up at the same time. But, I've noticed that the dates of the female rapes are quite close to the times when Seb Turner alleges that Fitch raped him. You made him tell you about the frequency and timing of the attacks when you took his statement. You got him to give you all the dates and times."

Billy ran his hand through his shock of blond hair, shaking his head as though finding the information difficult to comprehend.

"Come again, sir?" Billy peered at the boards. "Are you saying, what I think you're saying? That there's some correlation between the dates of Turner's rape and the rape of the women."

"Yes. I think that every time Seb Turner said he was raped by Fitch, within a few days there was an attack on a girl from The Goose."

Billy was silent for a moment, and then said, "Every time?"

"Every time, at least according to these boards."

Crane pointed in the general direction of the crowded whiteboards, which were completely covered with photos, dates, notes, ideas and details of reports available.

"So let's get all the files out. We need to double check this and if I'm right, see what we can do with it."

"Now, sir? But I'm going to the gym."

"Not now you're not, Billy. Phone your mate and cancel, while I phone Tina. It looks like we could be here for a while."

By 22:00hours Crane and Billy had tested the theory and were ready to make a list of things to do.

"So, Billy," Crane said, "if Seb Turner is our suspect for the female attacks, here's what we need to check. Write this down on a board as we go along," he instructed.

"One, get a composite picture of Seb Turner with black hair and one with blond hair. Two, see if any of the witnesses can identify him from those. Three, show them to Kim to see what she thinks. Four, get DI Anderson to talk to the police forensics lab and see if they have come across any finger prints or DNA on any of the items taken from the girls' flats or their bodies. Five, go to The Goose and show the composite pictures to the bouncers. Is there anything else you can think of?" Crane asked Billy.

"No, sir, not at the moment. We have Turner's fingerprints and DNA from his case against Fitch and we didn't come across anything incriminating when we looked through his room. It'll be a bloody shock if it turns out to be him though, sir. Never thought he was the type, you know?"

"Well, maybe the trauma he's been through has changed him. We can't really understand how he feels. Or understand what he's capable of doing now. Remember, this is all conjecture at this point. Although, thinking about it, he was starting to display anger if you remember some time back. Maybe he's so angry about what has happened to him, that attacking girls is the only way he can deal with it? Who knows? At the moment, we're not sure of anything, but at least we've a way forward, which is better than we had before. Anyway, that's it for tonight," said Crane rising and stretching, "we'll go and see Derek Anderson in the morning."

As Crane arrived home, the first thing he did was pop open a can of beer and sit in the kitchen on his own, savouring every drop. He hadn't expected Tina to be up, in fact had hoped she wouldn't be. She needed her sleep and the tablets from the doctor were helping. Opening the fridge, he spied a wedge of cheese and made himself some cheese on toast, while he drunk a second can. The kitchen was gleaming and as Crane wandered through the downstairs of the house, he saw everything was in order in the other rooms as well. He wondered who helped today and looking at the rota saw it was Jean Anderson. Once these two cases are over, they really must take Jean and Derek out for a meal, he thought, to thank them for all their support.

Before he slipped into bed, he checked on Daniel who was sleeping peacefully. Curling into Tina's back, he smiled at the thought that things were beginning to return to normal in the Crane household.

Chapter 41

When Crane and Billy arrived at Aldershot Police Station the next morning, DI Anderson was in his office, surrounded by files.

"You okay, Derek?" Crane asked Anderson from the door, as he was barely visible behind all the paperwork.

"What? Oh it's you, Crane," Anderson looked through a gap in the files. "Come in, as long as you haven't got more work for me. If that's the case, then you can bugger off."

Crane laughed as he moved into the office. "What on earth is going on?" he pointed to Anderson's crowded desk.

"Backlog in my paperwork," Anderson leaned back and threw the pen he was holding onto his desk. "Fancy a cuppa?" he suggested, standing and grabbing his jacket, not waiting for a reply. "I need to get out of here."

Once Crane, Billy and Anderson had moved to the mid-morning quiet of the canteen, and it was there that Crane brought Derek up to date with their theory from last night.

"Oh, God," Anderson shook his head, "that means

you have got more work for me."

"Well, not really, Derek, at least not to start with. First of all, can you get a police artist to have a go at putting blond hair and dark hair on this picture of Seb Turner?" Crane handed over the photograph. "Once that's been done, then we can re-interview the witnesses, show them the picture and I can also show it to Kim."

"And secondly?"

"Secondly?" asked Crane innocently.

"Yes, you said firstly. That means there's a secondly."

"Oh, right, well secondly, could you make a phone call to the forensics lab. I want to see if they finger printed all the victims' personal effects."

"Person effects?" asked Anderson as he stirred sugar in his cup of tea.

"Yes, sir," explained Billy. "We need to know if there are any finger prints on the handbags, belts, shoes etc. We're specifically thinking of anything the rapist could have touched before he put on his gloves and attacked the girls."

"He just might have been careless and touched something when he met them at the pub, or helped them out of the pub and into his car, after he'd drugged them. Our thinking is that he couldn't have worn gloves in the pub or going to his car, as someone could have seen him and thought wearing latex gloves suspicious," Crane finished.

"Mmmm," Anderson mulled over the request as he took a drink of his tea. "Alright, tell you what, if Billy here gets me a piece of cake to go with this cup of tea, I'll make some phone calls when I get back to the office."

As Derek's office had been taken over by his files, Crane and Billy returned to Provost Barracks to await the results of Anderson's phone calls. It wasn't not long before Crane heard from him.

"Right, Crane, I've got good news and bad news for you."

"Oh alright, give me the good news first then."

"The good news is that the artist can help with the photograph and if you come over tomorrow morning, I'll have copies for you showing Turner with both blond hair and dark hair."

"Thanks, Derek that is good news. So hit me with the bad news."

"The forensics lab didn't check the victims' personal effects for finger prints."

It's a good job Crane was sitting at his desk, otherwise he would have fallen over in shock.

"Not done them?" he managed to ask.

"No, it seems they concentrated on the flat itself and once they realised there were no stray finger prints and that the attacker must have worn gloves, they didn't go over the clothes or bags. You know how it is, backlogs, pressure of work, all those usual excuses."

"I take it you've asked them to go over the items now," Crane hissed.

"Yes, of course and they're giving them top priority. They're just waiting for the stuff to come over from storage and then they'll get right on it. But don't forget there are four cases to check, so you're not going to get any results today. Don't go phoning me every hour demanding answers. I've also scheduled CID personnel to go and visit the few witnesses we have in the cases - Becca Henderson's friend, the bar tender from The Goose and also Smith the van driver - with the photo-fits, to see if anyone can give us a positive identification."

"Very well, Derek. Let me know as soon as you hear anything."

Crane put the phone down before he shot the messenger and then escaped into the car park for a cigarette.

Crane managed to get home on time that evening and after changing out of his dark suit, he joined Tina and Daniel in the lounge. Tina was reading a paper and Daniel was chucking happily in his bouncing chair, which she was rocking with her foot.

"Hello, love," he said bending down to give her a kiss. "Had a good day?" he asked, although he could see with his own eyes that she had.

She was smiling, the baby was smiling and both those things made Crane smile. And if he wasn't mistaken, Tina actually had makeup on, just a smudge of lipstick and something that accentuated her eyes, but even those two small things made a big difference.

"Yes thanks," she answered. "Daniel and I went over to see Kim at Padre Symmonds' house. She seems a lot better, so we took a walk along Basingstoke Canal and had a bite of lunch at the pub afterwards."

"Well the change of scenery seems to have done you good as well. You seem a lot better yourself tonight and happier."

Crane held his breath as he realised what he'd said. The question was would Tina take it as criticism or a compliment?

"Glad you noticed," Tina said, her eyes flashing, but with merriment, not anger. "I am feeling better, you know. Those pills from the doctor and all the support

218

you organised has really helped. I'm probably not out of the woods yet, but I'm definitely getting there. Things don't seem as bleak as they did before and Daniel and I are getting along just fine, aren't we?" she looked down at the baby and smiled.

Daniel took this as his cue to make himself heard and started to cry. So Crane went to heat a bottle while Tina comforted the baby.

As Crane sat feeding Daniel, Tina picked up the newspaper she was reading.

"Look at this, Tom," she said and moved to sit down next to him on the sofa. She was pointing to an article in the Aldershot News with the lurid headline, 'Rapist on the Rampage!'

"Don't tell me," laughed Crane, "it's another insightful article from Diane Chambers."

"Looks like it. According to her, all women living alone have got to be extra vigilant when in their homes alone at night. She writes, 'Don't forget to lock up your houses and make sure this maniac can't get in. It doesn't matter if you live on the top floor of a block of flats; you need to be extra cautious as the Aldershot Attacker can strike anywhere, anytime!'"

"For goodness sake, she makes him sound like Spiderman. I'm sure she thinks she writes for a sleazy red-top, not the local weekly paper." Crane shook his head. "Any quotes in the article from the army?"

"Mmm, there's a bit here from Captain Edwards."

"Go on then, read it to me."

"Your reporter approached the army for an interview," Tina read, "but only a prepared statement was forthcoming, saying that at the moment there was no evidence to suggest that a member of the Armed Forces was involved in the case. However, when this reporter telephoned Captain Edwards of the Special Investigations Branch he said, 'It's beyond belief that a soldier would be responsible for these terrible crimes and I am urging Aldershot Police to make sure they do their jobs properly and pursue all lines of enquiry.'"

"Derek Anderson's going to love that one," hooted Crane. "I wonder what Edwards actually said. Diane Chambers isn't known for printing quotes verbatim. She definitely puts her own spin on them, as I know only too well."

"Is a soldier involved in these crimes?" asked Tina.

"I'm rather afraid one is," Crane said. "It's just that Captain Edwards doesn't know it yet."

Chapter 42

Time and tide wait for no man, so the saying goes. But in Crane's case it was a court-martial that waited for no man and the hearing had come around all too quickly, right in the middle of the further investigations in the civilian rape and murder cases. So instead of accompanying DI Anderson, going around showing the photo-fit to local taxi drivers, Crane was forced to wait impatiently outside courtroom No 1 on Bulford Camp.

Last Saturday evening had produced positive reactions from the bouncers on the door at The Goose. The two men regularly on the door on Saturday nights confirmed that they had seen both men entering the pub; the blond-haired man and the dark-haired one. However, neither could say which man had been there on which night.

Crane jumped up at the sight of Captain Lisa Nolan coming out of the courtroom and approaching him.

"Good morning, Ma'am."

"Sgt Major," the captain acknowledged him. "Right, we're starting with opening arguments and then we can begin presenting our case. You and Staff Sgt Jones are first on our witness list but at the moment I don't know if you'll be called before lunch or after. Where is Jones by the way?"

"Oh, he's here Ma'am. We travelled up from Aldershot together. He's just outside."

"Right you are," and as Captain Nolan turned on her heel and walked back into the courtroom, Crane made his way outside to join Jones for a cigarette.

They spent the rest of the morning walking around outside the modern one story building discussing various cases, in-between phoning Provost Barracks, gossiping about wives and other members of the SIB and the RMP and generally having a good old moan about having to hang around Bulford Camp.

As expected, their discussions turned to the Turner case and the evidence they would both give and from there, on to Crane and Billy's suspicions about Seb Turner.

"I don't suppose you found anything incriminating in his room in the barracks, did you?" Crane asked Jones.

"No, Crane sorry. What sort of thing did you have in mind anyway? I probably wouldn't have known anything was incriminating, as I wasn't searching for evidence that he was raping women."

"I see what you mean, Staff. Was there much in the way of personal effects in his room?"

"Just the usual. Let me think, oh yes, books, magazines, CDs, DVDs, clothes…"

"Yes, alright."

"Bank statements, pay slips, various medications, eye drops…"

"Staff!" Crane shouted. "That's enough."

"Well, you did ask."

Their altercation was interrupted by Captain Nolan

coming outside to inform them the court had recessed for lunch, so they may as well go and get something to eat.

Jones was called to give evidence after lunch, but Crane wasn't. Jones' testimony and the following cross-examination took longer than anticipated and as a result, Crane was fed up and exhausted by the time he got back to Aldershot Garrison, particularly as he had to return to Bulford again the next day, to give his evidence. After dropping Jones off at Provost Barracks, he made his way to the Padre's house.

Kim answered his knock on the front door.

"Hello, sir. Did you want the Padre? I'm afraid he's not here at the moment, he's taking Evensong at the Church."

"Actually, I came to see you, Kim," Crane replied.

"Oh, right, come in then, sir."

Over a cup of coffee, that Crane didn't really want, being awash with coffee from his protracted visit to Bulford, he told Kim about some new photographs he wanted her to look at and pulled out of his pocket a sheet of photos of 12 different men, including the doctored photograph of Seb Turner with dark hair. He slid it across the table so it was facing Kim, as she took a sip of her drink.

"What do you think?" he asked.

Kim cast her eyes down and after looking at the photos in silence for a moment, scraped back her chair and went to stand at the sink, looking out over the back garden. Crane wondered what was going on, but decided to keep quiet for the moment.

As she turned back to look at Crane, he saw beads of sweat breaking out on her forehead and her hands were shaking.

"Kim?"

Crane started to stand, but she shook her head and he sat back down without taking his eyes from her. She came back to the table, looked at her shaking hands and sat on them.

"It's that smell," she said, her forehead scrunching up in concentration. "Booze, that's what I think it is. I keep on smelling it. It comes out of nowhere. I can be doing something, reading a book, watching television and it just seems to waft past my nose. Sweat and alcohol and something else, something indefinable… oh yes, I have it now. It's the smell of fear. His or mine? I'm not sure, both probably."

Kim closed her eyes. Crane was motionless. He didn't dare break Kim's recollection, even though he was horrified by what she was going through in front of him.

"I can feel his hands touching me, tugging and dragging my clothes off," she continued, her hands breaking free of her legs and plucking at the white blouse she was wearing. "The cloth is ripping; buttons are popping, stockings tearing, hands probing, touching my bare skin. I can feel his weight on me. I can't move, can't stop the inevitable. Now I can hear him breathing. His hot breath is directly above me. I'm… I'm going to open my eyes and look at him."

Kim bent her head towards the photos on the table in front of her. Crane was mesmerised as she open her eyes and fixed on the picture of Seb Turner.

Chapter 43

Crane took up his position, once again waiting outside Courtroom No 1. This time the delay was legal arguments or something. In all honesty, he wasn't really listening to Captain Nolan's explanation. To give him something to do, he pulled his mobile phone out of his pocket and called DI Anderson.

Predictably Anderson was none too pleased to hear from him.

"For God's sake, Crane, I've got better things to do than keep you amused whilst you're waiting to give evidence."

"Stop with the histrionics Derek and tell me about 'blond streak' and 'white van man'. What do their statements say?"

"Well, both of them are fairly sure it's the same bloke. The barman from The Goose, the one you call 'blond streak' said he saw the man in our photo with dark hair with Kim. Smith, the white van man, has positively identified him as the man who asked him to deliver the rose to Kim. Although at that time he had blond hair."

"That's brilliant, Derek," Crane grinned but stopped

short of shouting, having to keep a bit of decorum and show some respect for the court building he was waiting in.

"Well, don't get too excited, Crane. As we've said before it doesn't put Turner in any of the girls' flats or give us any evidence that he raped or killed them come to that."

"I know, I know, but each identification inches us that bit closer."

"Well, we're not close enough yet, nowhere near in fact."

"Sgt Major Crane," a disembodied voice called from courtroom No 1.

"Sorry, Derek, got to go, I'm up. Speak later."

Crane's appearance at the court-martial was perfunctory, as expected. It was more a matter of what they'd found in Seb Turner's room, confirmation of the interviews Crane had with Fitch and affirmation that all procedures had been followed correctly. As he left the courtroom, the clerk was calling for Seb Turner. Giving evidence was intensely boring compared to the excitement of the initial investigation, Crane always felt. Still, it gave him an opportunity, after giving evidence, to have a quick word with the Justice Services.

Driving back to Aldershot Crane got a call from Derek Anderson.

"Hi, Derek," Crane shouted at the hands free microphone.

"It's alright, Crane, I can hear you, no need to shout," grumbled Anderson.

"Oh, sorry," Crane reduced the volume. "It's just I'm in the car and I'm never sure if people can hear me."

"I hear you loud and clear, thank you. Anyway, I've got news from the forensics lab."

"Excellent, go on then."

Crane changed lanes on the M3 to the slow lane, so he could concentrate better on what Anderson was saying.

"Well, they got two good finger prints, one off Madison's handbag and one from Kim's belt."

"Yes!" Crane punched the air and got a strange look from a lorry driver who was overtaking him. "Details?"

"Both finger prints are very clear, one index finger and one thumb." Anderson answered. "But…"

"But? Come on Derek, this isn't X Factor, drawing out the announcements to keep the suspense going. What is the but?"

"The prints don't match anyone in our databases."

"Great," replied Crane.

"Great?"

"Yep, send them over to my office. Now if you can, please. We'll check them against our records."

"Alright, but steady on, Crane. Just because we've found finger prints on the handbag and belt doesn't mean they are from the attacker. It doesn't mean they are from the same man. It doesn't mean…

"Yes, yes, I understand, Derek, don't go on. I'm not stupid."

"No, just headstrong, impulsive, blunt…"

"Thank you very much for that character assassination, but I need to go. I'll call you tomorrow.

"Crane!"

But Crane ignored Anderson, disconnected and immediately phoned Billy, arranging for him to check the prints against their records overnight.

Chapter 44

"Right, Billy, what have we got?"

Crane was in the office the next morning, eager to find out the results from the overnight finger print check Billy had run on the computer.

"You were right, sir, the prints belong to Seb Turner." Billy handed Crane a welcome coffee. "But that doesn't mean he raped Kim or raped and killed Madison, or any of the other victims."

"No it doesn't. But it puts him near them, talking to them, even in The Goose with them. What we now need is evidence that proves he is our suspect."

The ringing of Crane's phone interrupted their conversation.

"Crane."

"Sgt Major, Justice Services here. You asked us to call this morning."

"So I did. It's good news, we have a finger print match."

"Very well, expect a fax in about thirty minutes."

"Thank you very much."

Crane terminated the call and saw Billy looking at him with a wry smile.

"Boss?"

"The Search Warrant for Seb Turner's bedsit and effects will be faxed over in about half an hour. So go away and get a selection of evidence bags and sort out your forensics kit while we're waiting."

Billy dutifully went off to fulfil his orders, while Crane collected his files to present to Captain Edwards, thinking how much easier it was that SIB investigators were trained in forensic evidence collection, saving them time waiting for a specialist team to arrive.

He ran up the office stairs to the first floor, to deliver a report which was sure to make Captain Edwards' day.

A short time later, Crane and Billy were standing outside the room Seb Turner had been moved to, in St Omer Village.

"Are you sure he isn't here, boss?"

"Yes I'm sure. I called Captain Nolan and he's still giving evidence up at Bulford. The hearing ran over from yesterday afternoon apparently and the Judge adjourned the case until today because Turner got very upset giving evidence. He's going to be cross examined this morning by Fitch's defence team."

"Poor bugger." Billy went pink as he realised what he'd just said. "Sorry, sir, Freudian slip."

Crane grinned and then composed himself.

"Yes, well, let's leave out the sympathy shall we? He may have been very badly treated by Fitch, but it looks like he focused all that anger and projected it onto women, who he then raped and killed."

Billy unlocked the door with the master key given to

them by Aspire Defence Services, who run St Omer Village.

The door swung open to reveal a pristine room. The bed was made up with linen so sharp and clean the bed looked hard and uninviting. Very few personal effects were on display, just a small alarm clock radio and a picture of an older couple, who Crane guessed were Turner's parents.

"Seems a shame to make a mess," observed Billy.

"Yes, but make a mess we must, let's get on with it."

The room was so small that it felt claustrophobic with two men in, so Crane stepped into the small bathroom while Billy worked in the main room. He opened the bathroom cabinet and noted the usual things, shaving foam, razor, pain killers and such, dropping them into an evidence bag, together with a bottle of eye drops. He checked above and in the cistern of the toilet and tipped up the dirty linen basket, bagging its contents. There was nothing else to search in the room which was tiled from floor to ceiling.

Crane carried his evidence bags through to the main room where Billy was surrounded by his own evidence bags.

"Nothing incriminating here, sir."

"Where have you checked?"

"That cupboard unit - I've bagged the contents - and I've also searched the bed, but there's nothing hidden there."

The bed was now stripped of the starched linen which was lying at the foot of the bed on the floor. Placing his bags on the bare mattress Crane told Billy to get out of the way and moved towards the storage unit. Now empty, it was easy for Crane to turn upside down by himself. Taped underneath was a package.

Making sure he didn't do any damage, Crane slowly turned over the padded envelope. There were no markings on it. No address, no name, nothing. The flap was closed with a small brass clip, which Crane opened and looked inside the envelope. Drawing out a slim hard backed book, Crane placed the now empty envelope in an evidence bag which Billy was holding open for him.

Billy moved closer to Crane and they both read the contents of the slim volume.

Written in bold, childlike handwriting were letters, written but not sent, to Fitch, Billy and Crane, which were chilling in their stark honesty and intensity of feeling.

"Poor sod," said Billy, as he stepped back from the book and gazed out of the window. "You can't even begin to imagine what he's been through. Do you think he ever meant to send these as letters, boss?"

"Probably not, it was perhaps more a way of getting his feelings out, a cathartic exercise."

"Do you think he has raped and killed those girls?" Billy asked Crane, as he turned back. "Are we going to find anything incriminating?"

"Oh yes, Billy, we are. Just take a look at this one."

A Letter to Kim

My dearest Kim,

I think of you often. Do you think of me? I expect so, but probably not in the best possible light. This is a shame, as I did so want our relationship to work.

I saw you for the first time one day on the Garrison and followed you to Provost Barracks. From then on I kept returning to the outskirts of the Barracks in the hope of catching a glimpse of you. I was drawn to your beautiful hair, your demeanour and your confidence. But I didn't have the courage to approach you as I also saw your sergeant's stripes. So I just carried on watching from afar. Following you to work and back, out shopping, to the gym, to your parents.

I couldn't believe my luck when I saw you in The Goose. The fact that you were off-duty gave me the confidence to approach you. But as we talked I could tell you weren't really interested. You were just being polite. That's when I got carried away. I just couldn't help myself.

The anger just keeps building up inside of me, until it explodes. That's when I'm not responsible for my actions. That's when I just want to lash out. That's when I take what I need to prove I'm still a man.

Perhaps under different circumstances we could have been friends. Possibly more than that. Who knows?

Sorry.

Chapter 45

Crane and Billy both sat on the bare mattress in Seb Turner's room. To be honest, Crane wasn't thinking clearly. His mind was a maelstrom of thoughts. To give him some extra thinking time, he carefully stowed the diary in an evidence bag, making sure he filled out the slip on the front. Memories of Kim having a flashback, the post mortems he'd had to attend, hours spent looking at crime scene photos reverberated in his mind and he could feel his own anger building.

Determined to focus that anger, he said to Billy, "This diary will help with two things. One, extra proof, if needed, that Fitch was systematically raping and bullying Turner. And two, it also goes a long way to proving that Turner was Kim's attacker and stalker. But there's nothing else, nothing to tie him to Becca, Madison, or Summer.

"It doesn't even give us any evidence that he's the man that has been wearing wigs," said Billy. "Where the hell would he stash those?"

"Hang on a minute, didn't you say you met him in the gym?"

"Yes, boss."

"Come on, then, let's try his locker at the Sports Centre. The search warrant covers any place he would store personal effects."

They quickly covered the short mile from St Omer Village to the Sports Centre. As they parked in the car park opposite the main entrance, Crane was reminded of the hours he'd spent inside and outside this building, during the summer months. When he was in his own personal wilderness, acting as security liaison, watching over the Olympic athletes as they trained for the London 2012 Games.

This time there were no terrorists to battle with, just the staff who ran the Centre.

"We need to see the manager," Billy said to a spotty faced youth on the reception desk.

"He's not available," was the mumbled reply.

"Then who's in charge," Crane asked.

"Well, I dunno, me I suppose, until he gets back from his break anyway."

"In that case, I need the key to the locker used by Sebastian Turner."

"I can't give you any keys," the young man managed to shake his head and scratch a spot on his chin at the same time.

"I've got a search warrant," Crane thrust the copy of the warrant under his nose.

"I think you better wait until the manager gets back."

"Alright have it your own way," sighed Crane, having had quite enough of the boy's attitude. "I'm going to get into that locker with or without the key. Billy, lead on."

Crane and Billy left with the receptionist shouting after them, "Oy you can't, come back, wait…"

They pushed through the Men's Changing Room doors and Billy led the way through the maze of metal containers.

"This is the one," Billy pointed at number 269. "I've seen him use it loads of times, so I'm sure I'm right."

"That's good enough for me."

Crane nodded his approval and Billy got a small crowbar from the bottom of his forensics case. It took just a few seconds to prise the door open. Crane put on a pair of latex gloves and lifted out a sports bag, which was the only thing in there.

Billy spread out a plastic sheet on the floor so Crane could put it down. Slowly Crane unzipped the bag. There were three items in there. Two wigs, lying nestled together, one made of blond hair and the other dark brown, placed on top of a white plastic crime scene jump suit.

"Got you, you bastard," hissed Crane through his teeth.

Back in the car on their way to Provost Barracks, Billy asked, "How do you think he drugged the girls, sir? I wonder what he used and how he got it past the bouncers on the door of The Goose. They regularly do body checks to make sure there are no drugs being taken in.

After a moment, a smile broke out on Crane's face.

"Eye drops, that's how he got the drug into the drinks. It would also provide a legitimate excuse for a bouncer, should he get searched. Dry eyes that need eye drops or an eye infection that needs drops every few hours. I bet you both those eye drop bottles - the one we've just found and the one Staff Sgt Jones found in Turner's old room - will have traces of Rohypnol in them," said Crane as he pulled our his mobile phone.

Chapter 46

"The verdict of the court is *guilty*."

Crane watched from the back of Courtroom No 1 as Fitch blanched, swaying on his feet, before being held up by two RMP. As he was led away Crane turned to look at Private Turner. The young soldier was sitting down, his head in his hands, obviously weeping, his shoulders hitching up and down. Crane indicated to Billy that they should wait outside.

As Turner pushed through the door of the courtroom, into the corridor, Crane and Billy moved to greet him, stationing themselves one on either side of him.

"Well, done, Seb," Crane offered his hand, which the Private firstly looked at in horror and then gave a weak handshake.

"Great job, mate," Billy clapped Turner on the shoulder. "You must be so relieved."

"Yes, Billy, you've no idea…"

"Should think it lifts a big weight off your shoulders, knowing he's locked away and can't hurt you anymore," butted in Crane.

"Too right, sir." Turner's turned to look at Crane.

"Bet you're really proud of yourself," added Billy.

"Well, yes."

"Must make you feel good facing your fears, facing your tormentor," Crane said as he and Billy kept pace with Private Turner as they headed for the exit.

"Um…"

"A very brave thing to do that, identifying your rapist," Billy said as they jostled through the revolving main door and out into the dull, grey, mid-afternoon.

"Just like Kim," Crane added.

"Kim? What about Kim?" Seb stopped.

"So you know our Kim then?" Billy asked.

"Know, I…"

"Well you must do, otherwise you would have said, 'Kim who?' don't you think?" Crane said.

"Know? Kim? Well I suppose I must do."

"Where from?" Billy looked at Seb keenly

"Um…"

"Must have heard us mention her, eh lad?" Crane put in.

"Yes, yes, sir, that must be it." Turner was keen to agree with Crane.

"The thing is, though, I haven't. Mentioned her that is," Crane said as he gripped Seb's elbow. "Have you ever mentioned her, Billy?"

"No, sir, can't say I have," Billy replied and grabbed Turner's other elbow.

"In that case, I wonder how you know her? You do know her don't you?" Crane asked.

"Um…"

"You like her a lot, in fact, don't you?" Crane pushed. "It'd be nice to have a girlfriend like her, Seb."

"Yes, um, I mean, no, um…"

"I can see why you would need a girlfriend, mate,"

Billy adopted a conspiratorial tone. "To make you feel better about yourself. To make you feel a man again."

"Was that why you did it, Turner? Raped and killed Becca, Madison and Summer?" Crane growled. "To make you feel a man after that bastard Fitch violated you? Was it the only way you could get it up?"

"No - I - Billy, you can't think I killed them. Think that I would do something like that..."

Turner started struggling, but Billy and Crane held firm.

"Oh but I do think you killed them, Seb. You see we've found your wigs," Billy explained.

"I expect there'll be lots of your DNA on the inside of those. Oh and inside the plastic crime scene suit, don't forget that, Billy," added Crane.

"You're right, sir, we mustn't forget that."

"Wigs? Plastic suit? What are you talking about?" Turner asked Billy.

"I'm talking about items you wore when you raped and killed those three women, after drugging them first with Rohypnol from your eye drop bottle," replied Billy.

"And drugged and raped Kim, of course, we mustn't forget her," interjected Crane as they pushed through the door, stepping outside. Stopping Crane said, "Well, Kim, what you do you think? Is this him?"

Kim stepped from where she has been waiting on the grass to their left, resplendent in her army uniform, wearing her sergeant's stripes with pride, flanked by Staff Sgt Jones and DI Anderson.

"Yes, sir," she said addressing Crane, but staring at Private Turner. "That's him. That's the bastard who raped me," and she held Turner's gaze while Sgt Major Crane arrested and cautioned him.

Read on for an excerpt from Cordon of Lies.

Exemplo Ducemus

By example, shall we lead
Motto - Royal Military Police

Prologue

Some years earlier

The footsteps echoing through the underpass weren't hers. She was wearing trainers and the footsteps sounded like military boots. Stopping, she held her breath and listened to the drops of moisture falling through cracks in the concrete structure, their irregular tattoo sounding like gun fire. She inhaled the damp air, turned and peered into the darkness behind her, but couldn't see anyone. The grey gloom of early evening was glowing weakly, just visible at the tunnel entrance. Beyond that she could see the garish lights of the revered Tesco superstore she had left a few minutes earlier. Overhead she heard the faint rumble of tyres on tarmac, as cars hissed though the rainy night.

She tried to still her shaking hands by grabbing her bag and lifting it higher onto her shoulder. The end of the underpass, leading towards the relative safety of Aldershot town centre, was still some way away. As she started walking towards it, so did the boots. Matching her step for step. She broke into a run, her large bag weighing her down and banging against her hip. Her husband kept telling her not to carry such a big heavy bag and tonight she wished she'd listened to him. Her purse, umbrella, book and make up bag had turned into heavy stones, forcing the bag off her shoulder and down her arm. It landed with a thump on the concrete. She couldn't leave it behind, if nothing else she needed her purse, so she squatted down and retrieved the bag which had up-ended on the floor. With fumbling fingers she stuffed her purse safely back into the bag and began scrabbling for the rest of her stuff, scattered around her feet. Her lipstick had rolled away and looking around she saw it lying up against the wall of the underpass. As she reached for it, a black boot landed on her hand.

"Hello Carol," she heard over the snapping of bones, as her hand was ground into the floor.

If he said anything else, she wasn't aware of it. All she could feel was the extreme pressure of his boot and intense pain as the bones along the back of her hand cracked and crumbled. It felt like she was being been run over by a car, but whereas a car would move off her hand as it travelled on its way, Foster didn't liberate it, merely slightly shifted the position of his foot and placed it over her fingers. As he slowly pressed down on them, she blacked out.

When she came round he pulled her onto her feet from behind. His head was next to hers. His lips by her ear. The pain in her hand was abating, but she was incapable of moving it. She couldn't even wiggle her fingers and the shock of that realisation made her slump against Foster. He was muttering something and she strained to hear.

"Oh dear, have I hurt you Carol? Well now you know what it's like. You're feeling pain just like I did when you ended our relationship. The type of pain that fills your head, so you can't think of anything else. Well, I can't think of anything else apart from your betrayal. It just keeps going round and round in my head. I'm not able to do my job properly and it's all your fault. So I've got to get rid of you. Yes. That'll work. That'll get you out of my head."

"Barry, I..."

"I, what Carol? I'm sorry – is that what you wanted to say? Well sorry just doesn't cut it. You picked me up and then put me down, just like a plaything you'd grown tired of." His hand grabbed her chin, pulling her ear even closer to his lips. He hissed, "What was I, Carol? Just a diversion while your husband was away? A bit of fun on the side? Well, it's not bloody funny now is it?"

"No, Barry," she managed, hoping that if she tried to placate him, agree with him, he would let her go. But then she felt him release her chin and press something cold against her neck.

"Maybe I should just slit your throat with this dagger and leave you here to bleed out. That way, while you die, you'll have time to think about what you've done to me."

Carol swallowed, making the tip of the blade move slightly and dig into her skin.

"But your regret would be too little too late wouldn't it, Carol? So no, I don't think I'll do that."

Carol's relief was short lived as he continued, "I'll do what you did to me. Break your heart as you broke mine. That's more fitting don't you think? Breaking your treacherous heart?"

But she wasn't able to answer, only gasp, as the sharp point of his knife broke through her clothes and then her skin, pressing onwards through fat and muscle, towards her beating heart.

Chapter 1

Present day

Crane nimbly sidestepped the reporters crowding around the police barrier, ignoring their calls and questions.

"Sgt Major, any news for us?"

"Why are the Army being called in?"

"Can you comment on why a senior member of the Special Investigations Branch from Aldershot Garrison has been called to the scene?"

That last question came from Diane Chambers, self-appointed investigative reporter for the Aldershot News. In the light of Crane's previous tussles with the young woman, he simply shook his head and hurried away. He knew it was dangerous talking to her. Whatever he said to her made no difference; she either made it up, or distorted his quote to suit her article. So he kept his distance. Anyway, at the moment, the press probably knew more about what was going on than he did. Being an investigator for the Military Police, he'd responded to DI Anderson's terse phone call about 15 minutes earlier for him to "get his arse down here fast". And when DI Anderson of the Aldershot Police called,

Crane knew he had to move it. The local police and the military police worked closely on joint investigations, when the perpetrator or victim was military personnel. 'Down here' was the underpass walkway from the local Tesco Superstore, allowing safe pedestrian passage to the town centre, under the main road. Well, safe for most, Crane supposed, but not the victim.

Flashing his ID at the young constable on duty at the cordon, he walked to the entrance, where he stopped and called, "Derek!"

Anderson, an unwieldy, bulky figure in his crime scene suit, lifted his head at the interruption, then held up his hand in greeting and picked his way towards Crane.

"Thanks for coming, Crane. Here put this suit on and then follow me, walking…"

"Yes, yes, Derek, I know," said Crane as he pulled his way into the white suit, "walking in my footsteps."

"Sorry, force of habit," grinned Anderson, as he turned and guided Crane to the body of a woman, sprawled on the dirty floor in the middle of the underpass. There was a cold wind blowing through the tunnel, lifting Anderson's grey wispy hair from its normal position - covering his bald patch on the crown of his head.

"So, is she one of mine?" asked Crane looking down at the body.

"No, but she's the wife of one."

"Shit." Crane scratched at his well worn scar, just visible under the short dark beard he'd had to get special permission to grow. It covered the disfigurement that ran from his cheek to his chin, courtesy of shrapnel from an IED in Afghanistan, when he was training Afghan Military Police in investigative procedures.

A dead British Army wife was never a good investigation. The husband and his mates expected a quick result with all possible resources used, but his superiors wouldn't see it quite that way. A terrible thing to happen, for sure, but not a priority for the Army. It was effectively a civilian killed off-site, making it a police matter. Crane found it easy to empathise with the husband though and would do his best for him. God knows how Crane himself would feel if the victim was his wife, Tina. Breaking the news to the victim's husband would be hard, but someone had to do it and that someone usually meant Crane.

"According to information in her purse, her name's Melanie Green," stated Anderson, "and she lives, sorry make that lived, at an address on the garrison. Looks like she's was stabbed in the area of her heart, probably about an hour ago, according to the Pathologist. She was found by a local woman walking her dog. Luckily it was on a leash so we don't think there's been any contamination of the scene. When the dog walker realised what she'd found, she backed away from the body and ran to the entrance of the underpass, calling 999 as soon as she got a mobile signal."

As Anderson droned on, Crane squatted down to have a closer look at the dead woman. Actually dead young woman was nearer the mark. Crane guessed she was in her mid-twenties. She was lying on her back, her short blond hair in stark contrast to the black asphalt. Her head had dropped to one side, so Crane just had a view of a wide staring eye, half of her red painted lips and a gold stud earring. Her coat had fallen open, revealing a large dark red stain blooming on her snow white blouse. Her legs were closed and slightly bent at the knees. There was no immediate sign of sexual assault, as her clothes didn't look disturbed and all the buttons on her blouse were fastened correctly.

"Obviously we can't say if anyone else saw the body at this stage. It's likely someone did because of the time delay, but they decided not to call the police," Anderson finished.

"Mmm," replied Crane, who had been wondering what the motive was for killing Melanie Green. He pulled his attention back to Anderson and said, "Anyone who saw her probably didn't want to draw attention to themselves. Isn't this one of the places popular with drug dealers?"

"Yes," replied Anderson, "the lack of a CCTV camera makes it nice and safe from the prying eyes of the police. We've tried several times to get the council to install one, but no luck yet. We'll put out a call for witnesses later, through the press, and see if anyone comes forward."

"Well, there are quite a few reporters waiting for you back there," Crane indicated the barrier. "I expect they'll welcome a press conference or a statement from the police, they'll get precious little from the Army."

"Don't I know it," said Anderson. "You lot are tighter than a duck's arse when it comes to telling civilians what you're up to. Anyway I've just about finished here, so let's get going."

"Going where?"

"To break the news to her husband and interview him. The crime took place off the garrison, but the victim is the wife of a soldier. So as far as I'm concerned it's a joint investigation between the police and Army - unless you want me to handle it alone, of course."

Crane's colourful reply was drowned out by the rustling of Anderson's crime scene suit as he turned and walked away from the body.

Crane and Anderson often tussled over who a case belonged to. The military police were restricted to incidents which occurred on Aldershot Garrison, but Crane worked closely with the local police if an incident in their jurisdiction involved a soldier. Similar restriction applied to the civilian police investigating incidents on the garrison that involved military personnel. However the more serious the offence, the more the police had jurisdiction on the garrison.

Crane knew Anderson well, after working closely with him on several high visibility cases and both were respectful of each other's boundaries. Well, maybe not respectful, Crane thought as he followed Anderson, Crane being too pragmatic to pussy foot around authority. He had carte blanch to interview those of a higher rank than himself in the Army, whilst on active investigation, so he saw no need to treat Anderson or his colleagues any differently. What Crane wanted he usually got one way or another.

Back at the car Crane called Provost Barracks the home of the military police on Aldershot Garrison. He gave Staff Sgt Jones Mel Green's details and asked him to find out what he could about her husband, staying on the line while Jones looked it up on the computer. By the time Anderson and Crane had relieved themselves of their paper suits and boots and adjusted their clothing, Jones had the information. Crane scribbled down the pertinent details, resting his notebook on the top of his car, his mobile hunched between his head and his shoulder, trying to keep the pages from flapping in the increasingly blustery wind.

Jones told him the husband, Lance Corporal Green lived next door to Corporal Shaun Taylor from the same unit. Taylor was Green's direct superior, so Crane decided that was as good a place to start as any.

There was just one more thing to do, before Crane and Anderson could interview Green and that was to contact Padre Symmonds. If ever anyone needed a welfare visit, it was Green. As Crane waited for the Padre to answer the phone, his mind turned to how he would feel if he suddenly lost Tina. He was rather glad when the Padre answered and he was able to dispel those horrific thoughts.

"Good to hear from you, Sgt Major," the Padre said after Crane introduced himself.

"I'm afraid you won't think so when I tell you what's happened, Padre. I need pastoral and welfare support for a young soldier. DI Anderson and I are just about to tell him his wife has been murdered."

If Crane expected a gasp, or some sort of expletive, he didn't get one, merely a calm voice saying, "I'm so sorry you are having to deal with such an appalling situation, Crane. Give me the details and I'll come round straight away."

"Thank you, sir," Crane replied and did just that.

Crane and Anderson had a rather roundabout drive to Corporal Green's house, as they had to enter the garrison from Hospital Hill. During the journey Anderson asked Crane why he had involved the Padre.

"Because Army chaplains are now playing an increasingly larger role in the general welfare of soldiers. It doesn't matter if the lads are religious or not, the Padre is there to offer what support and comfort he can. It can be a harrowing situation, such as the one we have here, or mediating in a domestic dispute. Large or small, problems are increasingly being referred to the Padres."

"A bit like our family liaison officers, then, I suppose," said Anderson. "One officer is appointed to stay with the victim or their family for as long as they are needed."

"Yes, I suppose you're right," nodded Crane. "Here we are, Derek. We want Number 26 Williams Park; it must be on the even side, along here somewhere."

Crane parked the car and he and Anderson climbed out. As Anderson paused for a moment to collect a package from the back seat, Crane shivered and pulled the flapping sides of his coat together. The cold wind hadn't abated, filling the night with noise, as the trees were whipped first one way and then the other. The bleakness of the night reflecting the bleakness of Crane's message.

"It's this one," Crane pointed but started to walk up the cracked concrete path to number 28 instead of 26. He lifted his arm to knock on a gleaming black door, but before he could make contact with the wood, the door opened.

The two men stared at each other and before Crane could speak, the soldier standing in front of Crane said, "Oh bloody hell, it's the Branch!" using the well known euphemism for the Special Investigations Branch. Branch personnel are particularly distinctive, because they dress in dark, sober, civilian clothing, not uniform when on investigation and they wear their IDs around their necks.

The young soldier standing before Crane added, "Oh, sorry, sir, no offence meant."

"None taken," Crane smiled. He was used to the fact that that the one thing soldiers hated was a visit from the Branch, as it usually meant they, or someone they knew, were in trouble. On the other hand, a visit by Crane to an Army wife, more often than not meant the injury or death of a loved one serving abroad.

"Are you Corporal Shaun Taylor?" Crane asked.

"Yes, sir."

"We need to come in, there's a delicate matter I need your help with."

A few moments later, after Crane had explained the situation to Taylor, the three men stood outside the correct house, number 26.

"Ready, Taylor?" Crane said, as he saw the unhealthy pallor of the young soldier standing before him.

"Not really, sir."

Taylor coughed several times, as if the news that his friend's wife was dead was stuck in his throat, a blockage he couldn't get rid of, no matter how hard he tried.

"Look, lad, just be there for your mate, okay?" Crane said. "We can't break this sort of news to the man and then leave him on his own. I appreciate you haven't done anything like this before, but you don't need to tell him. We're doing that, okay?"

Taylor managed a nod in agreement.

"I need you to stay with him afterwards until the Padre gets here."

"Very well, sir," Taylor gulped, "I can do this."

"Right then."

The young man who opened the door looked at the three men stood in a ragged group along his equally ragged concrete path. He was dressed in civvies, a dark blue track suit complete with white polo shirt. His brown hair was shaved close to his head all over, a look favoured by many young soldiers.

"Sir?" Taylor asked, rubbing his hand over his bristly hair and addressing Crane. But without waiting for a reply, he turned to Taylor and said, "What's going on Shaun? What are you doing here?"

"Can we come in, Corporal?" asked Crane.

"Come in?"

"Yes, I'm afraid it's about your wife, Melanie."

"Melanie? Mel?" Green looked from one man to the other in confusion.

"I think its best we come in, sir," Anderson said showing Green his CID identification and together Crane and Anderson guided the bewildered Corporal through the house to the small sitting room at the back.

"Look," Green blustered, "what do you mean it's about my wife?"

Then he fell silent and stared at Crane and Anderson.

"Oh God, I've the Branch, CID and my direct superior, all together in my house. Something *has* happened to Mel hasn't it? Has she had an accident?"

"I'm very sorry, sir," said Anderson, "but a young woman fitting your wife's description was found dead earlier this evening, in the subway leading to the town centre. We found this in her handbag."

Anderson held up a driving licence with a picture of Melanie Green on it, protected by a clear plastic evidence bag.

"How? When? Look, it, it can't be her she's at her amateur dramatics rehearsal, I'm going to phone her on her mobile right now and sort this out, there must be some mistake. Maybe her purse had been stolen and it's someone else. There is, Shaun, isn't there? A mistake?" Green finished his garbled speech with a beseeching look at his friend.

But Taylor shook his head. "Sorry, mate, there isn't."

That denial made Green grab his phone off a small side table and start pushing buttons with fumbling fingers.

"Would this be the mobile you're ringing, sir?" Anderson interrupted.

Crane took Green's mobile from him, intending to stop the call, but he wasn't quick enough and all four men stared in horror at the bright pink mobile Anderson was holding, as it began to ring. After a flustered few seconds, Crane finally managed to cancel the call. He placed Green's mobile back on the table, as the man fell into a chair and began to cry. Crane watched in sympathy as the man's tears ran along each crease in his crumpled face. At a nod from Crane, Taylor moved around, squatted beside the chair and did his best to comfort his friend.

Sitting opposite the sobbing man, Anderson said, "Corporal Green, I'm very sorry for the loss of your wife, but we really need to talk to you."

"Talk?" was the muffled reply, as Green took the handkerchief proffered by Anderson, opened it and used it to cover his red eyes.

"We need to talk about your wife. The first few hours of an investigation can be vital, so I need..." at Crane's cough, Anderson amended that to, "so *we* need as much information as you can give us."

Green removed the handkerchief, hung his head and stared at the carpet beneath his feet, looking inward, adrift on the misery of his loss.

"Do you understand, Corporal?" Crane asked. He knew the man was falling apart, but Green didn't have the luxury of time for that. Crane and Anderson needed answers to the many questions they had and they needed them now.

As Crane's question provoked no response, he barked, "I said, I do you understand, Corporal?" hoping to break through Green's grief, reach the soldier inside of him and get his attention.

The ploy worked, as Green lifted his head, shrugged off Taylor's arm and stared at Crane for a moment, with something akin to hatred in his eyes. Crane didn't care about being hated, though. He didn't need Green to be his friend, just to help them as much as he could.

Green closed his eyes and mumbled, "Yes, sir, I understand. What is it you want to know?"

"Let's start with where Mel was going this evening and why she was in the underpass, shall we? Then we'll move onto where you were between 7pm and 9pm this evening."

Chapter 2

"Well, now we know why she was in the underpass, but not why she was killed," said Anderson as they walked back to Crane's car, after leaving Green in the capable hands of the Army Chaplin, Padre Symmonds. Crane shivered and pulled his coat on, over his self imposed uniform of dark suit and tie over a white shirt. He turned back and looked at the run-down row of Army houses they had just left, set amid weed infested cracked concrete paths and thought about the equally broken man they had just left.

"Green insists she was a model wife. That she didn't have affairs, or flirt with his mates, that sort of stuff," he said to Anderson, subconsciously scratching the scar underneath his close cropped beard. "But... he's only just got back from a tour of Afghanistan so, while the cat's away...." His voice tailed off as he looked at Green's front door and wondered if his attractive wife had taken solace in another man's arms while her husband was away fighting for his country. If she had, she wasn't the first to have done so and certainly wouldn't be the last. But did that behaviour warrant murder? He wasn't sure - but people had been killed for lesser crimes.

"Good point, Crane," said Anderson as he clambered into the car, bringing Crane's attention back to the present. "And Green hasn't really got an alibi, as he was home alone."

"When I've dropped you at the police station, I'll get on with interviewing Green's neighbours and friends as they're on the Garrison, if you do the amateur dramatics people," said Crane driving away from Williams Park back towards Aldershot Police Station.

"Will do," agreed Anderson. "You know, this case reminds me of one I covered a few years back, sometime after I joined CID at any rate."

"Bloody hell, how long ago was that? You've been in CID forever, haven't you?"

"I'm not old yet, Crane," said Anderson running his hands through his thinning, grey wispy hair, subconsciously proving Crane's point. "It's a cold case. A young woman was stabbed in the same underpass. She was the wife of a soldier as well. Never did solve that one and it's always bugged me."

"How long ago did you say?"

"I'm trying to remember, probably 10 years or so. We didn't get much help from the Army or their investigators on that one, I certainly recall that. Things were different then, I suppose. The Army was very good a closing ranks on civilians in those days. Even civilians in authority, such as the police. It's not like that now. Why we practically live in each other's pockets!"

Crane knew that Anderson was not only referring to their professional relationship. Crane and his wife Tina and become good friends of Derek and his wife Jean. The Andersons were particularly helpful when Tina suffered from post natal depression after the birth of their son Daniel. Thanks to Jean's help and support and that of the Army wives who lived in their cul-de-sac, Tina was now well on her way to recovery. Derek was also the only friend Crane had outside the Army. Living and working on the garrison meant that everything tended to revolve around all things military and it was easy to lose touch with civilian friends and acquaintances.

"Well, never mind that now," Crane said. "We've got a live case to solve. Your cold case needs to stay just that, cold."

As they pulled up at the police station Anderson said, "See you tomorrow for the autopsy."

"Will do. The Padre is taking Green to the Mortuary, so he can make the formal identification of the body first."

"Alright." Anderson got out of the car and waved to Crane as he walked through the doors into the police station, still looking distracted. No doubt worrying over his cold case, Crane thought. But Crane's priority was to get on with the new one, so before driving off he phoned Staff Sgt Jones, the man in charge of the Military Police boots on the ground and Sgt Billy Williams, Crane's normal investigating partner, to arrange for them to meet him at Williams Park and help him canvass the victim's neighbourhood.

Back in the CID office, Anderson looked at his watch. 10pm. He reasoned he might get lucky and find someone still at the West End Centre, so he called for two detective constables to accompany him, as it was highly likely there could be 20 or more people in the theatre group, too many for one man to handle. Together they walked the few minutes to the West End

Centre, known locally as 'The Westy'.

The Westy, a well known live music and theatre venue, had been opened as an arts centre in 1974. It was housed in a converted Victorian school house, which had been sympathetically renovated. The most striking features on the outside were the three separate frontages of the building. Each had a large rectangular window with a brick arch above. These were topped by a pointed roof, accentuated by white painted decorative wood down each side of the point. Anderson always whimsically thought they looked like gingerbread houses from Hansel and Gretel. At least there isn't a wicked witch inside here, he thought. On the other hand, he reasoned, there could be. A witch disguised as a normal human being, well, if amateur thespians could be called normal, he supposed. He shivered, not totally from the cold and pressed on. A sign on the wall advertised the play 'A Tale of Two Cities' opening in several days time.

Walking under the triangular, blue and glass dome entrance and pushing through the door, Anderson, flanked by his two younger colleagues, startled a young receptionist by flashing his badge and asking for the amateur dramatics group. She pointed to the large main doors of the auditorium.

"They're in there. Doing a dress rehearsal. What on earth's happened?"

The receptionist was certainly shocked by a visit from the police. It couldn't be him personally, Anderson decided. He knew he looked more like someone's friendly dad, than a police detective. His tweed sports jacket, receding gray hair and his penchant for sweet biscuits and cakes, of which he always had a ready supply, re-enforced the illusion.

He ignored her question and opened the theatre doors. The auditorium was in darkness with the stage dramatically lit, highlighting a bloody guillotine with a basket in front of it, complete with executioner. Walking across the stage, towards the guillotine, was a man dressed in a white flowing shirt and breeches.

"It is a far, far better thing that I do, than I have ever done," the actor said.

Anderson watched mesmerised, as the actor continued his speech, what Anderson assumed to be the finale of the play A Tale of Two Cities. Anderson had read the book many years ago and the only thing he could remember from it was that line, the one that opened and closed the book.

Kneeling in front of the guillotine the man placed his head on the block. "It is a far, far better rest that I go to, than I have ever known," he finished and as the guillotine dropped the theatre was plunged into darkness.

Anderson was stunned by the dramatic moment and a shiver fanned his back as he once more wondered if Mel Green's murderer was in the theatre. A jealous performer perhaps, hiding a dark secret. If so, his, or indeed her, acting skills were about to be put to the test under the close scrutiny of the police.

The spell was broken by clapping and cheering and as the lights both on the stage and in the auditorium came on, the cast spilled onto the stage, crowding around the lead player.

In a voice worthy of the actor he had just been watching, Anderson called, "Police - can I have your attention please!"

As the company slowly turned to face him and fell silent, Anderson continued, "Thank you. I'm DI

Anderson of the local police and I'm afraid I have bad news. A colleague of yours, Melanie Green, died earlier this evening on her way to this rehearsal."

There were collective gasps and a few sobs at the news.

"If you could all file off the stage and sit in the first couple of rows, my colleagues and I will come around and take your details and ask a few preliminary questions."

"What the…is this really necessary?" the lead actor they had just been watching said as he walked to the front of the stage."

"It's very necessary, Mr?"

"Hobbs, Michael Hobbs. As you can see I'm the principal actor here."

Anderson shook his head, afraid that this wasn't going to be an easy task, as Hobbs turned and indicated the cast, who were still crowded around him. He reminded Anderson of a regal rutting deer, surrounded by his doting does. Thespians were not Anderson's favourite people. He couldn't be doing with all the posturing and gesturing, which always grated. To Anderson, who was much happier calling a spade a spade, people like Hobbs were too affected for his taste. He sighed and hoped this wasn't going to be more difficult than it needed to be.

"I really must insist I'm afraid," Anderson said.

"But why? Is this really required? Just because someone has died."

Resolute in this thinking that firmness and fear was the best way of handling the actors, Anderson said, "Ladies and gentlemen, at the moment this is a request. However, if anyone feels they cannot assist the police, rest assured they *will* be arrested for obstruction. Mel

Green didn't have an accident. She was murdered."

A few gasps greeted his words, interspersed with comments of, "well really," and "how?" and even "why?" But Anderson was not to be shaken and the glare he directed at the assembled cast was enough to make them begin to do as he asked and a few people started to clamber off the stage.

"Can we get changed?" someone called.

"I need to get home." another said.

"How long will this take, Inspector?" a man with a clipboard asked as he walked out of the wings.

"As long as it takes, Sir. And you are?"

"Richard Moore, the Director."

"Well, Mr Moore, if you'll all do as I ask and stop asking me questions, we'll be able to get on with this a lot quicker."

"Oh, very well," Moore said. "Come along, everyone," he clapped his hands, "we better do as he says." Moore walked over to his lead actor and after a few heated words, Hobbs stalked off the stage.

Anderson called the two DCs over. "I want everyone's name and contact details, what they do in the theatre group and how well they knew Mel Green, if at all."

Anderson turned and looked around at the assembled cast. Some were still in costume from the dress rehearsal, some in normal clothes and a couple of men stood to one side, one of them being Moore. Hobbs had taken the centre seat in the front row and was surrounded by twittering women. Anderson decided they looked like baby birds, desperately fighting for attention, their heads back and beaks open, hoping for any tasty morsel their parent decided to toss their way.

Tearing his eyes away from them he said, "You two get on with this lot, I'll go and talk to Moore and that other bloke with him. One of you should start with Hobbs there. If you make him feel important he might have something useful to say." But looking at the man who was shaking his long black hair out of his eyes, he said, "Although maybe not. He looks as if the only person he's interested in is himself. Well off you go then," he encouraged and pushed the two young DCs in the direction of the cast.

Anderson moved over to talk to Moore. "Mr Moore and?" he looked questioningly at the other man.

"Gavin Lawrence, Producer." The man extended his hand and shook Anderson's.

"Ah, so you two are in charge then?" Anderson asked, looking at the two men who were dressed in immaculate casual clothes. Anderson wondered how they got such sharp creases in their trousers - he certainly never managed it.

"I wouldn't say 'in charge' inspector," replied Lawrence, emphasising his words with airy quotation marks. "But yes, we run things, I suppose. Decide what productions to put on, that sort of thing."

"Who deals with the auditions?"

"Well, that would be me," said Moore, looking up from the paper he was studying attached to his clipboard.

"Did Mel Green get a part in this production?"

"Well, yes, but only a very small one."

"Oh?"

"Well, shall we just say acting wasn't her forte? Oh, she was enthusiastic enough, always turned up, always happy to help, but acting? No."

"She didn't seem to mind not being picked?"

"No, not at all."

"Alright. What happened tonight when you first got here," Anderson continued his questioning.

"Well," Moore replied, "nothing different from our usual routine. We got here early, as we normally do," Moore indicated Lawrence. "It took about an hour to get everyone ready and then we did a complete dress rehearsal, running through the play with no breaks."

"Did you notice Mel wasn't here?"

"Well, yes, but it didn't really matter, she was only in the crowd scenes. We just got someone else to say her lines. She only had two as it was. I couldn't delay the dress rehearsal for her."

"Did anyone arrive late? Seem flustered? Preoccupied?"

Moore and Richards stole a glance at each other, looking horrified.

"You don't think anyone from here killed her do you?" said Richards.

"At the moment, Sir, we are exploring every possibility. Just normal police procedure. Nothing to worry about. But I do need an answer to my question. Did anyone seem different than normal when they arrived?"

"No, Inspector, not that we saw," said Moore speaking for them both.

"Very well. If you write down your names, address and mobile number, you can go and do whatever it is you do before you go home. I'll be in touch if I have any more questions."

Nodding, the men looked relieved and quickly wrote down their details, before rushing off back stage.

Meet the Author

I do hope you've enjoyed Honour Bound. If so, perhaps you would be kind enough to post a review on Amazon. Reviews really do make all the difference to authors and it is great to get feedback from you, the reader.

If this is the first of my novels you've read, you may be interested in the other Sgt Major Crane books, following Tom Crane and DI Anderson as they take on the worst crimes committed in and around Aldershot Garrison. At the time of writing there are six Sgt Major Crane crime thrillers. In order, they are: Steps to Heaven, 40 Days 40 Nights, Honour Bound, Cordon of Lies, Regenerate and Hijack.

Past Judgment is the first in a new series. It is a spin-off from the Sgt Major Crane novels and features Emma Harrison from Hijack and Sgt Billy Williams of the Special Investigations Branch of the Royal Military Police. At the time of writing the second book, Mortal Judgment has just been released. Look out for more adventures from Billy and Emma in the Judgment series in the near future. All my books are available on Amazon.

You can keep in touch through my website http://www.wendycartmell.webs.com where you can sign up to join my mailing list and in return get a free ebook! Everyone who signs up gets a free copy of Who's Afraid Now (kindle or pdf) a 10,000 word story which is a prequel to Hijack. Let me know which format you'd like and I'll email it to you, as a bonus for signing up. I'm also on Twitter @wendycartmell and can be contacted directly by email at: w_cartmell@hotmail.com

Printed in Great Britain
by Amazon